W9-BER-944

THE LAST
❧ OF EDEN ❧

❧ Stephanie S. Tolan ❧

THE LAST
OF EDEN

FREDERICK WARNE
New York   London

Excerpt from "To a Friend Estranged from Me"
by Edna St. Vincent Millay is from *Collected Poems*, Harper & Row;
© 1928 and 1955 by Edna St. Vincent Millay and Norma Millay Ellis.

Copyright © 1980 by Stephanie S. Tolan
Frederick Warne & Co., Inc.
New York, New York
Library of Congress Cataloging in Publication Data
Tolan, Stephanie S.
The Last of Eden
Summary: During her sophomore and junior years
at boarding school, Michelle must confront several
painful situations which make her realize the
place is not the "Eden" she once thought it was.
[1. Boarding schools—Fiction. 2. School
stories. 3. Interpersonal relations—Fiction] I. Title.
PZ7.T5735Ed [Fic] 79-22512
ISBN 0-7232-6177-6
Printed in the U.S.A. by Maple Press
Book Design by Kathleen Westray
1 2 3 4 5 84 83 82 81 80

FOR PAM,

 who knows what ends and what does not

❈ O N E ❈

When Mom turned onto Prospect Avenue and I once again saw Lake Huron that warm Sunday in September, it seemed almost as if I were coming back to Eden. The campus stretched out all green and rolling behind the old iron fence down to the ridge of white limestone breakwater. The buildings, their Gothic stone muted by ivy, seemed almost to be calling my name. It had been a summer of uncomfortable silences punctuated by yelling. We'd both tried, at first, to make our time together work, to pretend we were a family. But Mom wasn't up to coping with a teen-aged daughter she hardly knew, any more than I was up to coping with her or with a small town full of kids I hadn't been friends with since seventh grade.

I know how strange it must seem for me to call a girls' boarding school Eden, how strange that a fifteen-year-old might actually prefer that world of rules and religion and other girls to her own home. But after two years at Turnbull Hall its drawbacks seemed minor in comparison with the ghosts and shadows of the big white house Mom and I shared in the summer. And I know I wasn't the only girl at Turnbull who was really glad to be away from home, whatever that word might mean.

1

As we turned in between the stone pillars of the main drive, I tried to see who was already there. Scovie, Willie, Bits, Tag, and Jeannie would be back, of course. And Marty, my best friend, co-conspirator, and now my roommate. It seemed longer than a year since her father's limousine had slid to a stop in front of the dorm and we'd had our first glimpse of Martha Smithson Sheffield and her family. "The Princess," Scovie had christened her immediately, and the name had stuck.

And there was Miss Engles too, teacher of upper-school honors English, more understanding than the almost-stranger at the wheel of the car. It had been in Miss Engles' class that I first knew I was going to be a poet.

"What a relief to get the summer over with and get back to the people you care about," Mom said as she pulled into a space in the crowded parking lot.

I didn't rise to the bait, having learned over the summer that it was better to keep quiet.

Mom pulled on the emergency brake and sat for a moment, oblivious to the noise around us as girls shrieked and hugged each other and banged in and out of cars loaded down with suitcases and stuffed animals. "You might remember, Michelle, that it's a long year for me alone in that house."

I could have pointed out how much longer it would be with us there together, or how seldom she was alone anyway, with all the aunts and uncles and the men who appeared to keep a wealthy enough widow from pining away. But I didn't want another fight. I was too anxious to find the others and get unpacked, and anyway, I wasn't about to accept that particular load of guilt.

As I opened the car door and stepped out, it was pulled from my hand, and Willie, tanned and glowing after a summer at her father's ranch, hit me like a freight train. She threw her arms around me. "It's about time! How come people who live so close get here so late?" She pushed me away and looked at my straight hair, my T-shirt and faded jeans. "Didn't change a bit over the summer. Not even a decent tan! What's the matter, didn't the sun come out in Michigan this year?"

"Sure. I just didn't get out in it much."

Willie, except for her tan, hadn't changed either. Still the same bowlegs, the same short, wiry body in checkered shirt, jeans, and cowboy boots.

"Everybody else here?" I asked.

"Of course. You're late! My posters are up already, and Tag's halfway through her third fit about how little room there is for her. Scovie says she doesn't care about anything but getting the hard bed. Jeannie and Bits have new bedspreads and curtains. Bits made them over the summer, and their room is a knockout. And," she paused significantly and raised her eyebrows, "wait till you see what's new!"

"What?"

"You'll see. Emily Turnbull is probably rolling in her grave. Come on!"

Mom had opened the car trunk, and Willie grabbed a suitcase and headed for the dorm, leaving me to grab a few things and follow. She hadn't mentioned Marty, I noticed. Mother followed, bringing my small suitcase, looking stoical and resigned. The hardest thing about boarding school, I thought as I tried to keep up with Willie, who was bounding up the steps to the sophomore dorm on the second floor, was the coming and going.

We dumped my things on one of the beds in Marty's and my room, the last room on the stem of the T-shaped hall. Marty hadn't arrived yet. Then we went to the big room with the bay window where Tag was pulling a long mailing tube from her trunk and Scovie was taking practice swings with an obviously new hockey stick.

"Mike!" Scovie yelled, and dropped the stick on her bed before she ran to hug me. "Geez, where've you been?" She gestured at the room, the biggest on the sophomore wing and the only three-person room. "How's this for class? Window seat and all."

Tag unrolled a poster of zodiac signs and constellations and held it up to a space on the wall between two of Willie's horse posters. "The window seat is mine whenever there's a full moon."

"She *says* for meditating," Scovie said. "But personally, I think she's probably a witch." She cocked her head at Tag, whose long black hair, dark eyes, and olive complexion could give one that impression even if it weren't for the fact that she had an unnerving tendency to make predictions that turned out to come true. "I'm not at all sure I'm going to be safe living with her."

Scovie and I had roomed together the two years I'd been at Turnbull. We'd been put together by lot in the eighth grade, and it couldn't have been a better arrangement for me. Scovie's view of the world was almost unhealthily sunny. Give her a team to play on or a new sport to conquer, and she was satisfied. No, more than satisfied, she was downright happy. She liked to say that she'd been accepted at Turnbull because with all the brains there already, they needed a few athletic types to keep them on equal footing when they played hockey and basketball with other schools.

I can't imagine anyone else who could have made me care about anything at all that first year, when my life seemed to have disintegrated. Scovie hadn't been able to turn me into an athlete, to her great distress, but she had started the Daughters of Emily Turnbull—the D.E.T.s—enlisted its six members, and led the modest guerrilla warfare we'd maintained ever since against Turnbull's carefully ordered system. It was Scovie who had stolen the formaldehyde-preserved cat from the crock in the biology lab and draped it across a toilet seat in the lower-school dorm. We still fell apart when anyone mentioned Mrs. Jensen, our dorm mother that year, whose screams when she'd encountered that cat had wakened the whole dorm at four in the morning. Mrs. Jensen had left Turnbull after a year of the D.E.T.s.

And now Scovie would be rooming with Willie and Tag while I would room with Marty, the intruder, the Princess whom none of the D.E.T.s could understand. Tag had been the one to see that no matter how different Marty seemed to them, she and I had something in common that in some ways meant even more to me than the D.E.T.s. So it had been Tag who'd suggested that Scovie come in with her and Willie to request the three-person room. Nobody had said much about the change or the reasons for it. Scovie wasn't one to get her feelings hurt too easily. And now it was obvious that as far as she was concerned, our little band was not much the worse for the new living arrangements.

She grabbed for her hockey stick and held it up. "Do you see this, Michelle Caine? Do you have any idea what this means in hours of baby-sitting? I will never need to feel like poor white trash on the hockey field again! It was custom-made to fit the hands of Barbara 'Scovie' Scoville, the best center junior varsity ever had. With this stick we shall conquer the world!"

"These scholarship kids," Willie observed. "They get so excited over material possessions!"

"Only because we have so few!"

The honey-over-acid voice came from the doorway, and I turned to see Bits. It was all I could do to keep from gasping. The honey blond hair was longer and streaked by the sun, the smooth pink complexion and dimples that had made her notice-able even in lower-school days had become defined somehow. Her cheekbones were more prominent, and the effect was sud-denly much more than just pretty. Her figure, always good, had rearranged itself over the summer, and I knew once and for all that I would have to give up comparing my tree-trunk shape with hers.

"Have you seen *him* yet, Mike?" she asked. "You had to pass there to get here."

"Him who? Pass where?"

Before anyone had a chance to explain, my mother appeared behind Bits in the doorway. "Michelle, I'd really appreciate it if you'd hold off on the gossip until we've unloaded the car. I'd like to be back in Waterford before dark."

And so it wasn't until later, when Mom had left, that I learned about the Kincaids, our houseparents, and the apart-ment that had been made for them on the sophomore wing by knocking out the wall between two rooms. Marty had arrived at last, her belongings brought to the room by the chauffeur while the family spoke to Stoney, our headmistress. Then there were the formal good-byes, which I watched from our window: Mar-ty's father's stiff handshake, her stepmother's perfunctory hug, while her little brother Charlie hopped up and down around them until Marty bent down to give him a bear hug. She stood on the driveway watching as the long black car pulled away, then turned and ran for the dorm, bursting into our room mo-ments later. And it was from Marty, not Bits, that I first heard the news.

Donald and Priscilla Kincaid had come to Turnbull to teach and to be our houseparents—the first married couple ever to live in a Turnbull dormitory. Donald Kincaid would be the first male other than the chaplain to live on the school grounds in the whole hundred-year history of Turnbull Hall. Marty and Bits were ecstatic, each for her own reasons. The rest of us weren't so sure. But none of us could have known then how much their coming would ultimately affect our lives. That sunny September afternoon the clouds were already beginning to gather over Eden.

When I look back, I know that none of it was the fault of the Kincaids, or of the people who brought them to Turnbull, or even of Bits, or Sylva, who came later. That's what makes it so painful, maybe—not being able to lay blame. It's easy to accept the serpent in the garden as being evil. But it's not so easy to see that the destruction of something good can happen without any real villain at all. Or maybe there's a serpent in each of us, and nobody's personal Eden can last very long.

❧ TWO ❧

"How would you feel if Edna St. Vincent Millay or e. e. cummings came to Turnbull to teach English?" Marty asked, putting her underwear and socks into dresser drawers with an automatic quality that made it seem as if her body were somehow entirely separate from her mind. "It's like that! Priscilla Kincaid, teaching here! You should have seen Jane's face when Stoney told her that Priscilla Kincaid was taking Hamilton's place. If there had been any way to do it, she'd have taken me home then and there." Marty slammed the drawer and turned, her eyes practically glowing with triumph. "She'd have had trouble, though, explaining to Dad why the school that was so perfect last year had suddenly become all wrong. Stoney said they hadn't sent out news of the change because everything didn't get settled until the end of August. Thank heavens for me. If she'd had enough lead time, Jane would have come up with something and no telling where I'd be right now."

I plumped up my pillow and settled back on my bed. Mother had stayed long enough to get all my clothes unpacked, carefully arranging all my drawers as if I weren't capable of telling a sock from a bra without a diagram. I didn't mind because that got it done and kept her away from my books and papers,

8

which were more important anyway. And my journal, which I'd managed to keep a secret from her. If she even knew I kept one, she'd have been unable to keep her hands off it, and no one saw inside the covers of my journal except Marty and sometimes Miss Engles.

"I'm embarrassed to admit this," I said, "but I don't really know who Priscilla Kincaid *is*."

Marty shook her head. "You really are a cultural illiterate except in your narrow little field, you know. She is only one of the most respected young artists in the Midwest. She's had one-person shows everywhere that counts. One of her paintings can bring thousands of dollars already. One of them was even in that *Time* article about women in art."

"Okay, okay." I looked closely at Marty's face, the complexion usually so ivory-toned in contrast to the cap of short, dark curls. There was a tinge of pink to her cheeks and that sparkle in her eyes I'd noticed only when she was at work on a sketch or a painting she really cared about. "What I don't see is how you managed to make this happen. It's one thing to be a religious type, but do you have a direct line that makes God do exactly what you want?"

"You forget one of dear Father Purdy's favorite expressions, Mike. 'God works in mysterious ways.' Who'd have thought Jane herself would end up being responsible for getting me together with Priscilla Kincaid. I'll bet she's positively suicidal."

At that moment our door, which had been partly closed, burst open, crashing into the wall of Marty's closet. Jeannie Tucker hurtled in and threw herself heavily onto my bed. "It's the end of the world!" she moaned. "The seal of doom upon my very life! Woe!"

"Good Lord, Jeannie, what is it?"

Jeannie's round, pink face crumpled. "The Kincaids. Bits has gone right round the bend. You know the bedspreads and curtains—I bought the material and she sewed them over the summer. Do you realize she didn't even bother to take them out of the box? Didn't show them off, didn't tell me how long they had taken or how brilliantly they were made. You know the way she is about something she's sewn. If I hadn't taken them out and put them up, they'd still be packed. I even had to unpack her clothes! She's spent practically every minute since she got here hanging around their apartment."

"Why?"

"Why? Why? Does winter ask the wind why? Does the wave ask the lake? Haven't you *seen* him yet?"

"Who? Mr. Kincaid?"

Jeannie groaned and fell over backward. I managed to move my feet in the nick of time. She lay staring at the ceiling. "Donald Kincaid. Six feet four of looks that would put Adonis to shame! What does Stoney think she's doing? I am undone. Undone, do you hear? Bits just asked Scovie to change scholarship jobs with her. Woe!"

"So that's it." Bits' scholarship job had always been working in the kitchen, while Scovie did minor housekeeping jobs around the dorm.

"No more leftover eclairs! No more cake, no more cookies, no more stray bowls of pudding. Not so much as a half-melted Dixie Cup! I shall starve. I shall become a shadow haunting these halls forever in search of a morsel of food."

"Jeannie! Bits still has the key to the kitchen, the key to the food locker. It doesn't matter who works in the kitchen, just so we have somebody there. The Friday night parties won't end just because Bits is cleaning the dorm."

Jeannie sat up. "Maybe not, but all the other little treats will. She brought a leftover dessert back—sometimes two—almost every night for two years. How could I ever have made it through study hall without them?"

"Maybe this is the year for the ultimate diet," I suggested.

"Fat is beautiful," she answered. "I have my pride!"

"Well, can't you ask Scovie if she'd—"

"Are you deranged? Scovie wouldn't share an eclair with a starving puppy. The only difference between her approach to food and mine is that on her it doesn't show. Is it my fault that one look at a milkshake adds five pounds around my middle? Have you no sympathy for the handicapped?"

She was right about Scovie and food. Bits, on the other hand, had never been seen to eat a first helping of dessert, let alone a second. It had been one of the traits that made Bits and Jeannie such a good team. Like Jack Sprat and his wife.

Jeannie struggled up off the bed then, seeming to become aware of Marty's presence for the first time. She straightened the football jersey she always wore when she didn't have to be in uniform and squared her shoulders. "Never mind. I shall survive—somehow. Please pretend I never mentioned it at all." At the door she turned back. "By the way, did you get a look at *her* yet? Mrs. Kincaid? Weird!"

Marty waited until Jeannie was out of earshot before reacting. "Weird! Weird! I don't know. Maybe there's no hope for humanity at all. A person like Jeannie ought to be the last person in the world to judge somebody by appearances."

"What appearances? I haven't seen Mrs. Kincaid yet."

Marty looked down at her batik T-shirt and leather-trimmed French jeans. "Wait till you see her." She grinned. "You'll see what Jeannie means. Okay, I admit it. She does sort of dress the part of the artist. But that doesn't mean she dresses that way to be different, it means she *is* different."

"Just like you don't wear fifty-dollar jeans to prove how rich your family is."

"The thing is, I do wear jeans. You wear jeans. Bits and Scovie wear jeans."

"And Priscilla Kincaid?"

"Does *not* wear jeans! Still, a person with Jeannie's passion for culture ought to know better."

"Maybe she's an artistic illiterate like me. How many people here do you think know who Mrs. Kincaid is?"

Scovie came in at that moment, brandishing her hockey stick. *"Ta Dah!"* She turned to Marty. "It takes a hockey player to understand this stick, and I'm tired of the lack of respect I'm getting around here."

When Marty arrived at Turnbull, the first strike against her had been the money. Scholarship girls like Scovie and Bits were used to being surrounded by people with more money than they had. But Marty had been in a different league. Her father could have bought and sold the whole school twice over and given it to her for a toy. And at a school known for its high academic standards, where every student had been close to the top of her class wherever she had been before, the vastness of the Sheffield wealth had given rise to the suspicion that her father had bought Marty's way into Turnbull. I think there were a lot of people who wanted that to be true. So when she turned out to be bright enough to take over my place at the top of our class, I wasn't the only one who was shaken. Marty had quickly proved to be what Bits called the "perfect Turnbull girl," rich, bright, religious, and, as Jeannie had added, thin. When she made the junior varsity hockey team, she had solidified the antagonism. No one was allowed to be good at everything.

But over the year Scovie and Willie had begun to accept Marty, at least as an athlete. They couldn't deny her natural ability, and they couldn't help but respect that and her willingness to work.

Scovie was still extolling the virtues of her hockey stick and glowing with pleasure at the fact that it had actually cost more than Marty's when the supper bell rang. "Geez! I forgot I'd traded with Bits. I'm late for work!"

As she tore down the hall, Marty shook her head. "That's a basic difference between Scovie and Bits. Scovie honestly doesn't mind having to work to be here."

"Why should she? In her family everybody works. She'd be embarrassed to take anything she didn't earn."

Marty sighed. "I like Scovie, Mike. If only I knew how to make her understand that."

"I don't know. She's the one who named you the Princess, remember. And it isn't an image that's easy to break."

As we started for the dining room, I noticed a flicker of something in Marty's face, something that didn't fit her calm, controlled approach to life. But it was gone so fast, I couldn't be sure I'd really seen it. I was left, as usual, wondering whether Marty needed anything or anybody outside herself. "Me," I assured myself. "She needs me." And I was no more certain of it than ever.

❧ THREE ❧

The first weeks Marty was at Turnbull, if someone had predicted that she and I would become friends, let alone "best" friends, I'd have suggested they apply to the nearest loony bin. My place at Turnbull was secure. I was second in command of the D.E.T.s, and my grade-point average put me first in our class.

Marty was a stranger, a "new girl." But she arrived with more than the trappings of a limousine and chauffeur and mink-draped stepmother. She didn't seem to have any of the usual new-girl nerves. Most kids on the first day latch on to anyone who speaks to them. Some cliques formed that day last straight through graduation. The Princess spoke to no one, but managed to give the impression that her aloofness was purely her own choice. Later, much later, I learned the truth about that. But at the time, no one saw anything except that calm face, that posture, that almost casual elegance that people really do connect with royalty. Or aristocracy, anyway.

And then, when I hit the first real snag of my academic career, Latin, it turned out to be Marty's particular favorite. Day after day I listened to her answer questions with a certainty that drove me mad. Latin was such a struggle for me that I had to give up the ambition I'd had since fourth grade to be an archaeologist. How could I study ancient cultures if I couldn't even learn Latin?

So the D.E.T.s took Marty on as a particular enemy. We went out of our way to make her uncomfortable—from silly pranks like short-sheeting her bed to stealing her homework papers. But nothing we did seemed to shake her. We had no way of knowing what was going on underneath until, out of the blue, she struck back. With a casual and apparently innocent reference, she let our dorm mother know about a stone-skipping contest we had organized on the breakwater, the one utterly forbidden area of the campus. People have been washed away by Lake Huron waves, and there is a constant fear that some student will be lost on the breakwater. Most of us pay no attention to the rule, but we make sure we're never caught.

Our punishment for endangering lives with that contest was to miss the all-school picnic. I doubt if any of us will forget the smile on Marty's face as the bus pulled out of the parking lot, leaving the D.E.T.s with a full day of window washing ahead of us.

Tag, the quietest D.E.T., had said little about Marty, but she'd been watching her more closely than the rest of us. It was Tag who observed that the Princess was unusually religious. Every Turnbull student must go to chapel before school every weekday and twice on Sunday. Turnbull is high church Episcopalian, complete with incense and plainsong and a Mass every morning for anyone who gets up early enough. Marty went to early Mass every feast day, even on Saturday, our one day to sleep late. That trait alone was enough to alienate us. Combined with everything else, it condemned her absolutely and provided the seed of our revenge.

I was the one who planned and organized it. After all, I was the one who could be deposed from my place at the top of the class. And it worked even better than I'd hoped. One Sunday, during choral Mass, Jeannie arranged to sit in the front row of the choir, where she could get the full impact of the acolyte's enthusiastic incense swinging. Jeannie has a terrible allergy to incense, and in moments she was bright red, gasping for breath and blinking against a flood of tears. I "helped" her from the chapel, left her in the dining room, and went up to Marty's room, a single, where I set up a kind of shrine. I had bought votive candles and a perfectly ghastly poster of Jesus with lots of thorns and blood at a religious store in town and had stolen a censer and incense from the sacristy the night before. I made Marty's desk into an altar, lit the incense and the candles, and by the time church was over, was back in the dining room being solicitous of poor Jeannie.

Willie and Scovie cornered Marty as she came out of chapel and kept her talking while our dorm mother had a chance to get back to the dorm, where clouds of incense were pouring out into the hall. By the time she'd notified Father Purdy, who was in a rage about the stolen censer, Marty hadn't a chance. Turnbull expects its girls to be upstanding Christians, but ever since an epidemic of religious fervor overtook a class a few years back and girls began reporting visions of saints in their rooms at night, Father Purdy had kept a strick lookout for fanaticism. Marty was forbidden to attend any chapel service that wasn't required and had to report to Father Purdy twice a week for what she later described as "deprogramming."

The D.E.T.s celebrated the success of my plan with an unusually big feast of goodies stolen from the kitchen. But, for me, the elation wasn't to last. One morning before breakfast

Marty appeared in Scovie's and my room with the rolled-up Jesus poster and handed it to me without a word. How she knew I'd been the one, I still don't know.

A few days later, I found myself by chance in the same pew as Marty in morning chapel. As we began to sing the final hymn, I happened to glance her way and saw that she wasn't singing. She was just holding the hymnal and looking down at the floor. At first, it was as if I felt from her more than the silence of not singing. It was a silence from deep inside herself, as if she were holding something in too hard. Then I saw the tears in her eyes, and for the first time in my life I considered the possibility that someone might be genuinely religious. Until then, I'd thought that anyone who went to chapel more than they had to was just trying to impress the faculty.

It was probably my own background that made me feel that way. We'd always gone to church. It was part of being in the social structure of Waterford. But when the catastrophe happened, when my father and brother were killed in the accident, we hadn't been able to get much comfort from St. Matthew's. Some obscure idea of heaven could not take away the pain of waking up to that emptiness every morning. Mom and I had each handled that pain differently, or hadn't handled it. But we had stopped going to St. Matthew's.

Marty's religion was something new to me. I went to Father Purdy that very day, took the blame on myself, and ended up being campused for the rest of the semester while Marty was freed from the deprogramming and allowed to go back to church whenever she wanted. The D.E.T.s pronounced me insane. As time passed and Marty didn't so much as thank me, I began to agree with them.

A few weeks later, on a Saturday afternoon when everybody

else was in town, I came back from sulking on the breakwater and found the marble bust of Caesar from the Latin classroom standing in the middle of my desk. Around him were votive candles, flickering in their cut-glass cups, and two sticks of drugstore-variety incense, scenting the room with sandalwood. I was too stunned for a moment to react. And then, as I began to laugh, I heard the sound from across the hall of Marty's door clicking shut.

For a week the school was in an uproar over the disappearance of Caesar. Mrs. Hershberger, the Latin teacher, threatened the entire student body with eternal flames, while Caesar lay hidden under my bed. The D.E.T.s immediately suspected that a rival organization had sprung up, and Scovie and Willie set out to try to find out who they were.

For some reason, I didn't tell anyone. And when I got a note signed *The Masked Gladiator*, suggesting that Caesar should return to Rome at midnight, I kept that a secret too.

By the time Marty and I had carried that statue through the dark classroom wing in our pajamas and bare feet, hiding in a storage closet while the security guard passed, the Princess had gone forever. From that time on, when Marty answered Mrs. Hershberger's questions with such certainty, I had only to look at the bust of Caesar and I felt better.

Eventually, the "Masked Gladiator" offered to help me get ready for a Latin test. Eventually, we began to spend evening study hall together in Marty's room, first because of Latin, later just to talk. Eventually, I began to write my poetry and Marty drew and there it was. I was still a D.E.T.; I still had a whole portion of my life that was separate from Marty. But as what she and I shared became more important, the other things couldn't help meaning less. By the end of the year, our becoming roommates seemed inevitable.

❦ F O U R ❧

Every year, the first day of classes is preceded by an assembly. It's Miss Stonehill's yearly chance to explain the philosophy of Turnbull Hall, prod everyone to great academic achievement, and introduce the faculty. One at a time, they're introduced, the two elderly gentlemen and the "gray ladies," as Bits calls them. It isn't that Turnbull teachers aren't good at what they do. Most of them are, or the school wouldn't have the reputation it does. It's just that, thanks to Stoney's insistence on "appropriate dress," they all tend to look more alike than the girls in their uniforms. Miss Engles, looking like a refugee from a rural commune, had always been the only teacher who got away with looking different. Her flannel shirts, corduroy pants, and walking shoes had always made her a standout during the introductions. This year, however, she was to be entirely eclipsed.

When the time came to introduce the Kincaids, Miss Stonehill drew herself up to her full six feet, composed her angular features into that granite expression that had given her her nickname, and began, her clarion tones reaching the very back of the assembly hall. "We believe in keeping Turnbull Hall in contact with its time as far as is reasonably possible, without emulating a world in which change is more and more a euphe-

19

mism for chaos." There was a slight shifting among the new girls who weren't used to Stoney's speeches. She paused and peered out across the room where the entire student body was gathered, two to a seat in the large, old-fashioned desks. The shifting stopped. "As you know, the pressures on schools like ours to go coeducational have been eased somewhat of late by the feminist movement. Nevertheless, we feel that for too long certain role models have been lacking here. Adding a married couple to the faculty will provide one such role model. Mr. and Mrs. Kincaid will serve together as houseparents in the sophomore dormitory wing. More than ever, Turnbull will be a family."

When the Kincaids stood up, there was a collective gasp that seemed to be half amazement and half appreciation. Jeannie had exaggerated Donald Kincaid's looks a little, but only a little. Standing next to Stoney, he seemed to tower over her, and the combination of dark wavy hair, blue eyes, and broad shoulders was breathtaking. Priscilla, on the other hand, was of medium height and thin almost to the point of emaciation. Her long brown hair was pulled into pigtails and she wore boots, dark tights, a peasant skirt and blouse, and a shawl draped around her narrow shoulders. In her ears were enormous golden hoops strung with wooden beads and feathers.

Stoney listed Priscilla Kincaid's accomplishments with a kind of reverence she usually reserved for Emily Turnbull herself. I wondered if anyone but Marty even partially understood the significance of that list. "Weird!" I heard Scovie whisper behind me. I glanced sideways at Marty and saw what I had never seen before. Marty was blushing.

When Stoney announced that Donald Kincaid would be teaching American history, Marty leaned over and whispered in my ear, "Watch for a sudden jump in the popularity of *that* course."

I glanced at Bits, who was sitting across the aisle from us, staring at Donald Kincaid with glazed eyes, and nodded.

Then it was time for Father Purdy's spiritual pep talk and the benediction. As always, he had on his tweed jacket with the leather elbow patches, over his black shirt and clerical collar. He emphasized every other point with one of his huge collection of pipes.

As he issued his invitation to anyone who felt the need of spiritual counseling to visit him in his study, Marty leaned toward me again. "He knows more about vintage wines than about helping people," she hissed. She had never told me about those few sessions she'd had with him before I'd confessed to our hoax, but she was as close to bitter about Father Purdy as I could imagine Marty being.

❦ ❦

The blush in assembly that morning was the beginning of a series of amazing breaks in the Princess's cool. Marty, who had put up with all our harassments without flinching, Marty, who had continued to draw and paint despite having been sent to a school with no emphasis on art and a mediocre teacher, Marty, who ignored the D.E.T.s obvious snubbings, was suddenly as jumpy as a kitten. I watched in amazement as she barely touched her lunch, as she sat through Mrs. Hershberger's Latin class with a vacant expression and no answers.

Writing poetry was important to me, more important than anything else I could think of. The couple of hours a week I had spent with Miss Engles our freshman year, waiting with sweaty palms to hear what she had to say about my newest masterpiece, had been important too. But art seemed to be much more than that for Marty. As if it absolutely shaped who she was and how she reacted to everything around her. With Priscilla Kincaid living at the other end of the hall, Marty was suddenly leaping around the room like a mad person. I noticed that her hands were shaking after dinner that evening as she was gathering up her sketches and putting them into her portfolio.

"Come with me, please!" she begged.

"Why? Do you mean to tell me the Princess is scared?"

"Terrified."

"I don't see why. You can't be afraid she won't like your stuff. Even Stoney had to admit you were too good to waste your time with freshman art last year."

"Wouldn't you want me to go with you if you were taking a poem to e. e. cummings?"

"Of course, you idiot. He's dead."

"Don't be funny."

I looked from the shaking hands to the face, where a faint tinge of green was beginning to color the ivory. "Okay, okay. I've never met a famous artist before. Maybe I'll learn something that'll help me contend with you."

꒳ ꒳

As Priscilla Kincaid looked through the pages of Marty's portfolio there was a silence broken only by the comings and goings in the hall outside the door. I looked around the apartment at the huge abstract paintings, which I assumed were Mrs. Kincaid's, at the hanging plants, and at the Indian cotton throws covering old Turnbull furniture. There was little resemblance between this apartment and the old dormitory rooms that had been combined to create it. In the middle of the living room was a bay window—a duplicate of the one in Scovie's room down the hall. This one, however, overlooked the lake. The horizon was beginning to go gray as the sun set behind the school. I watched the fingers of clouds change color as the lake darkened and wondered why the Kincaids had come to Turnbull, why they had left Chicago for a little town like Graylander, with nothing to recommend it but quiet. The lake view didn't count. They'd had Lake Michigan in Chicago. Marty had said that Mrs. Kincaid's paintings could bring thousands of dollars each. She certainly didn't have to teach high school students for a living.

It occurred to me that, smart as Marty was, her obsession with art could blind her to other things. She was so excited at the chance to study with Mrs. Kincaid that she never stopped to ask why such a famous person would be burying herself at Turnbull Hall.

When she had finished looking at everything in Marty's portfolio, Mrs. Kincaid put everything back except the charcoal sketch of Marty's brother Charlie, the first of Marty's sketches I'd seen and still my favorite. There was something in those few lines that made Charlie seem to come alive, to leap right off the paper. It was looking at that sketch that had made me see for the first time the similarity between Marty's art and my poetry. The sketch was like a poem without words, an echo that stays even when you close your eyes. We were both trying to share something from so deep inside it was like creating a direct circuit from one mind to another.

Mrs. Kincaid looked at that sketch for a moment, then looked at Marty, still without saying anything. Marty's hands were clasped tightly in her lap—to keep them from shaking, I guessed. But she looked directly back at Mrs. Kincaid with one of her best Princess expressions.

Mrs. Kincaid smiled finally. "I'll look forward to working with you."

Marty mumbled a very un-Princess-like thank you and blushed again. Twice in one day.

"I have only one question. Why did you come here instead of finding a school with a serious art faculty?"

Maybe all artists weren't so engrossed in their own work that they didn't notice anything else, I thought. Here was my question, only backward.

Little by little, Marty had told me the story, but she didn't talk about her family willingly, so I was surprised when she told it all so directly now. "My mother was a painter. A good one, I think. I don't know why she married my father. Maybe it was his money. Or maybe she wanted the social position. Anyway, Dad isn't interested in art at all except as an investment. He never did understand her need to work. He didn't like her traveling to shows, he didn't like the hours she worked in the studio. I guess he figured she'd give it up when children came, as if it were some hobby or something. But she didn't. They fought a lot when I was little, but they didn't get it solved. Then, after my brother Charlie was born, the fights got worse. And she left."

The story had appalled me when I first heard it. How could a mother leave her own children? But Marty had never seemed to hold it against her.

Mrs. Kincaid didn't even seem surprised. She touched Marty's hand briefly, her long, thin fingers with the plain clipped nails scarcely more than brushing Marty's. "Do you see her often?"

Marty shook her head. "Hardly ever. Charlie probably wouldn't even know her if he saw her." She looked out the window at the lake, which was now a deep slate gray. "By the time she left, though, something had gone out of her painting. There hadn't been any shows for a long time. She doesn't paint at all now." She sighed. "I guess I don't blame her for leaving, but if she had to go, I wish she could have made the break in time to save her work."

"That might have been before there was a Marty," Mrs. Kincaid said, smiling. "Perhaps that would have been more of a loss for the world than her painting."

Marty went on to explain that there had been a divorce and that her father had remarried—a woman much more like him than her mother had been. From the moment Marty had shown any interest in painting, her stepmother had done everything she could to discourage her. Jane had always claimed that she wanted to save Marty from an insecure, irresponsible life. "But I think she's afraid it will remind Dad of my mother. I applied to the Wellington Academy, and they accepted me. I still have the letter from the headmaster that says they particularly wanted me to come. But Jane convinced Dad that Wellington wouldn't be 'well-rounded' enough. She knew Turnbull, so she convinced Dad that I should come here. The strong academic environment was supposed to be good for me. There was nothing I could do but come."

Mrs. Kincaid handed Marty her portfolio. "Nothing worthwhile is easy, they say. That's how you learn whether it's really worthwhile or not. Besides, here we are, you and I. Fate works in strange ways. We'll work very hard this year and you'll be well-rounded too!"

As we walked down the hall toward our room, anyone else

would have seen the same old Marty, calm and casual. But I knew those eyes.

The moment we'd closed our door, Martha Smithson Sheffield actually threw herself onto her bed. "Did you hear what she said? She looks forward to 'working with me.' Not teaching me, not even helping me. *Working with me!*" Then she was up and pacing.

When the bell rang for study hall, I got out my journal to record this amazing day. As I started to write, Marty was still too excited to sit down.

⁕ F I V E ⁕

Miss Engles' classroom is one of my favorite places at Turnbull. Bookshelves completely cover one wall—she likes to keep
her own favorite books around her instead of trusting them to
the library, she says. Besides, I think she wants to keep books
in front of us every minute, one way or another. Another wall
is mostly windows and radiators, the windows looking out
across the front of the campus, the gardens and stone fountain
and trees along the iron fence in the background. Above the
blackboards on the other two walls are portraits of Byron and
Shelley and Poe and Dickens and Shakespeare and all the authors high school lit courses usually deal with, plus a few pho-
tos of contemporary authors that she changes every few
weeks—"since we don't know yet which ones will last." Sitting
in that room you are always being watched—the eyes of poets
and novelists and playwrights are on you all the time. I never
know whether that's going to make me feel good or wretched.
It depends on how things are going.

"Well, Mike, I've read what you wrote over the summer, and
there are some good things here."

I was sitting in one of the tablet armchairs, pulled close to
the desk. Miss Engles was leaning back in her swivel chair, one

foot resting on a partly open drawer, my poetry in her lap. It had taken me most of freshman year to get over my fear of taking her something new, and that horrible wait as she read it, a slight frown that I could never decipher puckering her forehead.

"If you let Miss Engles scare you out of writing, you don't want to be a writer anyway," Marty had said one memorable day when a poem of mine had actually provoked Miss Engles into suggesting that maybe I should give it all up. "You wouldn't want her to say good things about something she didn't think was good. What point would there be in that?"

Marty had been right, of course, and I'd gone on with those after-school meetings. Eventually, I'd come to realize that the days when Miss Engles really liked something made it all worthwhile. If she never criticized, her praise wouldn't have meant anything. But this was another year. I'd had a summer away, writing without any feedback, and I was terrified all over again. I wasn't ready, yet, to look her in the eye, so I stared at the picture of Lord Byron, with his aristocratic sneer.

"There are some good things here," she said again.

I grinned and looked at her, only to meet those calm, cool gray eyes, and feel them go straight through me.

"But I think it's time you got away from Millay and cummings and Frost and got in touch with the world you live in. Poetry isn't something that stopped twenty years ago, you know. And there's nothing wrong with copying another poet's style. You can learn a lot that way. But these people are dead, and I want you to start reading some other poets. Get away from the books and find some little magazines. That's where the life is today. The library subscribes to a few, and I can lend you some others. Still writing in your journal?"

"Yes." I was looking at Byron again.

"Good. Write some things besides poetry now. Try some stories. Do an article for the newspaper. Get inside the language
and see how many different things you can make it do for
you."

Did she mean my poetry wasn't any good?

"Have you ever tried essays? Not like themes for class, but
essays, writing that tries to persuade or teach or follow some
new line of thought."

"Just what you assign for class."

"Well, then, try some. Get some good examples—E. B.
White or George Orwell, for instance—and read them. Spread
out a little. You're beginning to repeat yourself."

She handed me the folder of poems, and I took them, thinking how much nicer it would have been to spend this time getting smashed by a hockey stick on the field with Scovie and
Willie.

"Mondays okay with you?" she asked.

"You mean you're not trying to get rid of me?"

She slammed the drawer with her foot and sat up. "Michelle
Caine, how do you ever expect to survive as a writer if you in-
sist on walking around without your skin? Get a little confi-
dence. Are you going to curl up and die with your first
rejection slip?"

My hands were sticking to my folder. "I hadn't planned on
getting any," I said, and stood up.

"That's better. How's Marty?"

"Are you kidding? She hasn't touched the ground since we
got back."

Miss Engles stood up and walked me to the door, where she
leaned against the blackboard. "She's got herself a minor miracle. Let's hope she's able to use it. And Scovie?"

I shrugged. "Who knows? She's the same as ever."

"Thank heavens there are Scovies in the world!"

As I walked back to the dorm, clutching the folder full of poetry I somehow didn't like anymore, or trust, I thought how nice it would be to leave one of those sessions with Miss Engles being sure I knew what she was talking about. And I wondered how I was going to write an essay. What a terrible idea. How could anybody get interested in essays?

On the way back to the room, I stopped at the library to find a book of essays, but I wasn't hopeful.

When I got to the room, Marty wasn't there, and I knew she was still in the art studio. "It's not fair!" I said in the general direction of Miss Engles' classroom.

Over the next two weeks I said those words on the average of ten times a day. Some of the essays I read weren't bad, but it wasn't the same as poetry. I couldn't think of a plot for a story, couldn't think of a subject for an essay, and hated the idea of writing for the paper. If it hadn't been for my journal, I might have stopped writing entirely. Marty dropped out of junior varsity, much to Scovie's and Willie's disgust, so she could spend some time in the studio every day after school. Mrs. Kincaid had started her working on abstracts, and she would come back to the room before dinner absolutely glowing. "It's like a whole new world," she'd say. I'd sit at my desk with a book of essays open in front of me and snarl.

It began to seem almost like the days of the D.E.T.s before Marty. Scovie and Willie would be at hockey practice, Marty in the studio, and more and more I'd spend the whole time between the end of classes and dinner with Jeannie and Tag and Bits, eating, talking, goofing off. I didn't feel as if I were getting anywhere, but at least it was comfortable.

"I don't care what any of you say." Jeannie was sitting on my beanbag chair, her uniform blouse as usual untucked, her knee socks crumpled around her ankles. "It's an invasion of privacy. It's probably unconstitutional. You practically have to put on a formal to go to the bathroom at night!"

Bits was combing her hair for the third time since she'd come in, making pouty faces with her lips and turning her head this way and that in the mirror over my dresser. "You don't need a formal." There was an edge to her voice that was there more and more often. "A bathrobe would do."

Jeannie didn't seem to notice Bits' tone as she shifted her weight in the chair. "We didn't have to wear a robe every time we set foot outside our rooms when Mrs. Clawson was our dorm mother. She wouldn't have cared."

"When was the last time you went to the john in your bra and panties?" Bits asked. She had a point. Jeannie would have to die before she'd be seen in her underwear.

"That's what I mean. See how limiting it is? What if I felt a sudden urge to change my personality? What good is adolescence if you can't experiment? Suppose I suddenly had an overwhelming desire to become a nudist? There's Mr. Kincaid lurking everywhere."

"He doesn't lurk, for God's sake! He lives here!"

Jeannie pulled a bag of M & M's out of her skirt pocket and ripped it open. "Doesn't he? And you live right outside his door with a dust mop in your hand."

Bits pulled herself away from the mirror. "It happens to be my job to keep the hallways clean."

"Curious how you keep that end of the hall so clean while this end gets knee deep in bunny fuzz!" Jeannie put a handful of M & M's in her mouth and crunched them, looking steadily at Bits.

"It so happens that Mrs. Kincaid thinks I do a pretty good job. She asked me to clean their apartment for her once a week. For money! She doesn't have time."

Tag, who'd been lying on Marty's bed, apparently absorbed in a science-fiction book, looked up.

"I never knew you were so crazy about housework," Jeannie said, and aimed the empty brown bag at my wastebasket. It missed. "I haven't noticed that passion around the room!"

"For money," Bits repeated. "Some of us need it more than others." She looked at Marty's dresser, where a bottle of Joy perfume sat, unopened, under the mirror. "We can't all bring hundred-dollar-an-ounce perfume with us to boarding school!"

There was no mistaking her tone now, and I found myself doing what I always tried to avoid. "Her father gave that to her as a back-to-school present. What was she supposed to do, give it back? It isn't her fault her father has money."

"Maybe she'll let you use some for the Southport dance," Jeannie suggested. "Dan would be impressed."

Bits frowned. "I may not go."

Tag looked up from her book again. "Dan too young for you?"

Bits' face reddened and she looked away. "It's just that military academy boys seem so silly in those monkey suits. After the guys I met this summer, I mean."

Turnbull exchanges dances with Southport Military Academy, fifty miles south of Graylander. At the first dance of our freshman year, when we were all given blind dates according to height, Bits had been paired with a buck-toothed kid with huge, owlish glasses. Within half an hour Dan Peterson, the leader of the junior honor squad, had cut in on them, and the blind date was over. Bits had spent the rest of the year gloating over that conquest. There was never a question of who she would be with at a dance. They were all but pinned.

Jeannie rolled her eyes at Tag. "Guess whose picture isn't on the dresser anymore. And guess whose last passionate letter is moldering unanswered on whose desk."

Marty came in then, bringing with her an aura of turpentine. Bits glowered at her and flounced out.

"Even more gracious than usual," Marty observed. "What have I done now?"

Jeannie heaved herself out of the beanbag chair. "Theoretically, it has to do with a scent a bit more elegant than turpentine." She followed Bits.

Tag closed her book and looked at Marty. "It isn't you. What's wrong with Bits hasn't anything to do with perfume. And it couldn't be fixed by a *case* of Joy." Tag flipped her single long black braid over her shoulder and stood up, her dark eyes troubled. "Stoney was wrong this time. It isn't going to work."

When Tag had left, Marty shrugged. "I sure am good at clearing out a room!"

"It's just as well," I said. "I'm supposed to be writing a stupid essay. I could use some quiet time."

"You've got it. I need a shower before dinner."

I sat for a while, my notebook open in front of me, and thought about what Tag had said. She meant the Kincaids, obviously, but I couldn't believe it was anything serious. After all, Bits wasn't the only one who had a crush on Donald Kincaid. There had been popcorn parties in the Kincaids' apartment the first two Friday nights, and the whole class hadn't shown up just because of a passion for popcorn. On the other hand, it didn't usually make sense to ignore Tag. She had a way of be-

ing right. Maybe it was her Greek blood. Jeannie claimed she
was descended from an oracle. Tag said it wasn't magic, it just
came from shutting up and watching.

This time, though, she's exaggerating, I decided. I'd fallen
under Donald Kincaid's spell myself. He would sit on the
couch in their apartment and talk, or sometimes play the guitar, and it was nice to sit there and listen. Half the time I didn't
remember later what he'd been singing, just how he'd looked,
leaning over his guitar. It was true that Bits was usually the
one who managed to sit next to him on the couch or else directly at his feet, but that was only because she was persistent.
After all, Bits was fifteen, and no matter how pretty she was,
there was a heck of a difference between fifteen and thirty.

As I sat there, thinking about Mr. Kincaid and the way it felt
to be near him, listening to him sing, a poem began to put itself
together in my head. I looked at the page in front of me where
I'd crossed out three different beginnings for an essay and
shrugged. I wanted to be a poet, after all, not an essayist. So I
went to work on it.

> *Your eyes are like a forest*
> *where I walk a while*
> *before returning to myself.*
> *I keep this pine cone that I found*
> *to look at sometimes,*
> *to touch,*
> *a promise of other forests*
> *where I may one day live.*

"You'd think gray eyes would be dull," I wrote the next day
in my journal.

I took the poem to Miss Engles instead of an essay, and when she finished reading it, her eyes changed. They were like the lake when the sun is going down and it gets violet and blue with sparks of light against the waves. "This is more like it," she said. "This doesn't come from someone else's poetry, this comes from you. When you can write a poem that's as honest as this, you must write a poem."

I went over her reactions as I wrote in my journal later, trying to understand the difference between this poem and the things I had taken her from the summer. I could see what she meant, but it wasn't entirely honest either. It was about Donald Kincaid's eyes, but only the way they were when he was singing. I liked to look at him. Everybody did. But I didn't know how I felt about him. I couldn't stand him in class. He would read all the time, either from the book or from those 3 x 5 cards. It was as if he didn't trust his teaching. History was dull enough without sitting in class day after day listening to somebody read. In class his eyes weren't the same at all. In class they were closed, and nobody could get in.

But that poem was a beginning. I began to write poetry again and even found I could manage an essay once in a while. The newspaper published an article I did about Mrs. Kincaid's work. It was almost as if something had clicked in my head, and things were going right again. Between Marty's painting and my writing, we had formed our little island again.

Despite Tag's fears, Stoney's idea seemed to be working. As the semester wore on, there really did get to be a difference in our class. There seemed to be more class spirit. Cliques, which tended to be exclusive, to break a class into factions that competed to cut each other out, seemed almost to dissolve. We began to have a feeling that really was like a family. Despite the title "dorm mother," the women who ran the other dorms had never been much more than guards. There were always a few girls who got along with the dorm mother, but mostly she was seen as an adversary to be outsmarted. The Kincaids were more like friends. The door to their apartment was usually open, and everybody felt free to go in and watch television or just talk whenever they wanted to. People began to hang around the dorm, not just because it was the only place to go, but because they liked it there.

Mr. Kincaid began Saturday afternoon bike trips down Prospect Avenue to the public beach a mile away. We'd take hotdogs and marshmallows to roast on a bonfire, hunt for treasures in the sand, play Frisbee. Mrs. Kincaid didn't go along because she spent her Saturday afternoons in the studio, doing the work she didn't have time for during the week. Marty stayed with her. And the hockey teams usually had games. But most of the rest of us went.

I'd take my journal and go off by myself as soon as we got there. Jeannie claimed the exercise was good for her, choosing to ignore the fact that once there she did nothing but consume hotdogs and marshmallows. Bits, who had always spent Saturday afternoons in town, haunting the little shops whose cheapest item was beyond her reach—"They see the Turnbull uniform and never notice I don't buy anything"—rode next to Mr. Kincaid, laboring to keep up on one of the school's old three speeds while he pedaled his ten speed effortlessly. We'd get back around dusk, and sometimes he and Mrs. Kincaid would take a few girls into town to a movie later. It was a good time.

My fifteenth birthday came on a Sunday. Mom came down to take Marty and me out for dinner to celebrate that afternoon, and we actually had fun. Mom gave me the typewriter I'd been hinting for all summer, and Marty gave me a portrait of me she'd done in pastels.

"When did you do this?" I asked, amazed at how she could manage to make it look like me, but better. "I never saw you working on it."

Marty grinned at Mom and shook her head. "When she's writing, she doesn't notice anything. I did it during study halls, of course. Luckily, you never bothered to ask what I was working on."

"It's beautiful," Mom said. "I'd like to have one like it."

"I'll do one for you, but a little different, I think. In this one I was trying to get the way she looks when she's working on a poem. Too much of her face is hidden for a regular portrait."

That's what I liked about it, the way she made it look as if I were really doing something, not just staring into space the way people usually are in portraits. My hair was falling over my face like it always does, and I was leaning my cheek on one hand. But Marty was smart enough to know what Mom would like. I thought she'd probably do okay for herself once she started trying to sell her work if she could read people the way she read my mother. But then she probably didn't want to be a portrait artist any more than I wanted to write essays.

When we got back to school, Marty went off to find Mrs. Kincaid, and I stayed by the car to say good-bye to Mom.

"She's a good artist," Mom said.

"I told you that!"

"Best friends aren't always the best judges."

"Well, with Marty it's pretty obvious."

"Yes."

Mom looked at me very hard, and I half expected some sort of criticism. I thought maybe we'd gotten along so well during dinner because Marty had been there, and Mom was too polite to start complaining in front of her.

"She says you write pretty well," Mom said.

"I . . . " I didn't know what to say, so I just nodded.

"Then I'm glad I got you the typewriter. And I hope you'll use it."

"I will. You know I will. Thanks."

"I think Marty is good for you, Michelle." She leaned over and gave me a peck on the cheek. "Happy Birthday. See you at Thanksgiving. We're going to be at Monica's this year."

And then she drove away, without a word about how lonely she was or how lucky I was that at least I was someplace I could be happy or any of that. As I scuffed through the leaves on the way back to the dorm, I wondered if I could get Marty to come with me whenever I went home. It certainly seemed to help my relationship with Mom!

When I got back to the room, I put the pastel on my bulletin board, opened the typewriter case, and set the typewriter in the middle of my desk. All in all, it had been one of my nicer birthdays.

"The noble experiment seems to be working," Scovie said one rainy afternoon at the end of October, as we stood looking at the dorm bulletin board. The sign-up sheet for the class hockey team was full, and five people had signed up to be cheerleaders. "We certainly do have class spirit! We're the only class whose team was full the first day." Her voice changed. "Of course Marty's name isn't here."

"She doesn't want to give up her studio time for hockey practice," I explained.

"Of course not. Not the great artist. But J.V. hasn't been as sharp without her this year, and the sophomores really *need* her. The seniors are going to be tough."

"She's a traitor, that's all," said Willie.

I remembered when they'd resented her for being so good at hockey. "Listen, the cheerleaders will make a huge difference. We're the only class with a cheerleading squad!"

"Cheerleaders!" said Willie in disgust. "You'd think we were Graylander High. Can you imagine a Turnbull girl wanting to be a cheerleader?"

"Snob!" Scovie punched Willie in the arm. "You're just knocking it because you know how dumb those bowlegs would look under a short skirt."

Willie punched her back, and they went off to their room, scuffling as they went. I stood there for a moment, looking at the list of cheerleaders. Bits was captain. It had been her idea to have cheerleaders in the first place. She was designing the outfits and making them herself. Designing and making clothes had always been her specialty. "Poor women have always had to sew," she'd say, but she hadn't fooled anyone. It was Bits who had sewn secret pockets into the lining of all the D.E.T.s blazers so we could carry notes and stuff from the kitchen under the noses of the faculty. I wondered what the cheerleading costumes would be like. And why she'd decided the class needed cheerleaders in the first place.

As I turned away from the bulletin board, Marty came up behind me, grinning like the Cheshire Cat.

"What's up?" I asked.

She didn't answer, just took me by both arms and marched

me to our door. When we got there she flung it open, and there were the old votive candles on my desk, their light flickering on a cream-colored envelope. In the upper-left-hand corner a quill pen was drawn in black ink, and my name was written across the center in Old English script.

I just stood there, unable to get my breath, looking at the envelope. "Impossible!" I thought. "I'm just a sophomore!"

"I found it there when I came in and decided it deserved the candles."

"And where's the incense?" I asked, surprised that I could talk at all.

"Well, are you going to open it or just stand there staring at it?"

I didn't need to open it. It was an invitation to join Penwomen. An invitation that didn't go to sophomores.

"It happened once before," Marty said, as if she'd read my mind. "The other person who made it as a sophomore wrote two best sellers later."

I picked up the envelope. "My books will be far too literary for that!"

And then I was crying. "How strange," I thought. "Marty paces and I cry."

❦ SIX ❦

The first few weeks after I'd been asked to join Penwomen I practically lived for Sunday afternoons. The meetings were held in Miss Engles' apartment on the top floor of Faculty House. It was different to see Miss Engles in her own apartment, but everything seemed to fit her. It was all bare wood floors and bookshelves and big, comfortable furniture. My favorite place was an old red leather armchair, but whoever got there first usually took it since everybody else liked it too. Someone would read a story or a poem and then we'd talk about it. Sometimes I'd spend all week working on something to take to the meeting and then decide at the last minute not to take it. I'd just sit and listen and eat cheese and crackers and wish I had the nerve to read a poem. But it didn't take me long to get into the discussions. They were really ferocious sometimes. But they were good, too.

One of the best things about going to those meetings was having an excuse to be off campus alone. Sophomores usually can't go out unless somebody else goes along, but since I was the only sophomore in Penwomen, an exception was made. Faculty House was only across the street and down the block, but I would leave early and take a walk along Prospect Avenue before I went to the meeting. The Kincaids just let me have the afternoon to myself on Sundays. I hadn't felt so free since I'd been at Turnbull.

As the class hockey tournament got closer, excitement mounted all through the upper school. Varsity season was over, and the class teams were out practicing every afternoon, wrangling over which class got the field most often. The finals were to be held the Saturday before Thanksgiving. Southport boys were coming for the afternoon game and staying for dinner and the Hockey Dance, the only informal dance of the fall semester.

The campus had gone over into winter by then, the leaves long gone from the trees, the weather alternating between cold rain and light, blustery snow.

Two games were to be played Saturday morning, freshmen against sophomores and juniors against seniors. The winners of those games would play for the school championship in the afternoon. As the bleachers filled around the hockey field that morning even I had caught some of the excitement. The halls of the dorm were covered with posters prophesying victory, and the Friday night popcorn party at the Kincaids' had been a pep rally, complete with Bits leading the cheerleaders through all their cheers. Everybody knew that a sophomore win was at least a reasonable possibility.

Marty and I sat together and tucked a blanket around our legs against the wind off the lake. Priscilla Kincaid, in a long coat and fur-lined boots, joined us. Mr. Kincaid was score-keeper, so he sat at the officials' table on the sidelines.

"I'm afraid I don't know as much about this game as I should," Mrs. Kincaid admitted, declining Marty's offer of a corner of our blanket. Snow flurries were beginning to blow lightly across the field. "But everybody says we're going to win."

"This game, at least," Marty agreed. "The freshmen could barely scrape up a full team. But we may have real trouble this afternoon, if the seniors win their game."

"They will," I said. "The whole forward line is made up of varsity players. Our only hope is exhaustion. They play the second game this morning and won't have much time to rest."

"Exhaustion and stage fright," Marty added. "The seniors' center forward is pinned to a Southport cadet, and half the other members of their team are going with someone. Nobody knows what having the guys here will do to their game."

"Won't that cause us problems too?" Mrs. Kincaid asked.

I laughed. "Not our class. Most of us are still having blind dates. You'd be surprised how many cadets there are that nobody wants to see twice. Bits is the only one who's actually going with somebody from Southport. And she's only a cheerleader."

Mrs. Kincaid nodded. "Having a boy friend here to watch could only make her better at that!"

I wondered if I'd imagined a touch of irony in her voice. Bits is only fifteen, I reminded myself. But when the cheerleaders came out on the field in their tight sweaters and short skirts, I noticed that Mrs. Kincaid's lips were set in a tight, thin line.

Bits looked fantastic. Our class colors were orange and blue, and she had chosen the orange for the sweaters. It seemed almost to add brightness to her gleaming blond hair. The blue and orange striped skirts barely covered the blue panties they wore underneath, and there was a surprising amount of bare leg above their orange knee socks. I shivered and wondered how they were going to keep from freezing. The wind wasn't strong, but it seemed to cut right through my winter jacket. All it appeared to do for Bits was to brighten her cheeks and give her knees a glow to match.

"They'd better keep moving or they'll freeze like a bunch of orange popsicles," Marty said.

It occurred to me that if Bits and Mrs. Kincaid stood side by side, wearing bathing suits, for instance, the comparison would not favor Mrs. Kincaid.

Then the whistle blew, the teams took the field, and I forgot everything except watching Scovie as center forward and Willie as goalie while our team ran over the freshmen like a freight train. My two years with Scovie hadn't been entirely wasted. At least I'd learned to appreciate good playing and moves that were perfectly timed, with a grace I knew from experience couldn't be learned. Marty shouted encouragement and yelled her approval for every good move they made. She really did love hockey, and I could tell she was wishing she could be out there with them.

I was the only D.E.T. not involved in the game somehow. Tag was playing right wing and doing a decent job. Jeannie, whose weight didn't keep her from being fairly fast on her feet, made a creditable fullback. Of course, they didn't consider *me* a traitor for not playing. With a hockey stick in my hand I'm a running catastrophe. I sometimes wonder how I even survive gym. And no one even suggested I try cheerleading.

After we won, Marty and I went down to congratulate the team.

Scovie, sucking on an orange slice, thanked me for my cheering. "Mike, I heard you over everybody when I made that last goal," she said.

"It was a great play!" Marty said.

Scovie went on as if Marty weren't there. "Of course this afternoon will be different. We sure could use some more front-line strength." She went off to join the other team members to change clothes before the second game.

"Maybe she didn't hear you?"

"It's okay," Marty said. "From her point of view, I'm letting the class down." She looked at the sky, still full of heavy gray clouds. "The snow may have stopped, but I'm cold. You want to skip this game?"

I shook my head. "We're supposed to stick around and give the juniors and seniors a full house."

She handed me the blanket. "Maybe so, but there's just enough time before lunch to finish what I've been working on in the studio. I'm going to lose this afternoon and this evening and I really want to get done. See you at lunch."

When I went back to join Mrs. Kincaid and told her where Marty had gone, she nodded. "Good. The painting she's working on now is really fine. It's something new for her, and she's excited about getting it finished."

Halfway through the junior-senior game, with the seniors leading by a comfortable three points, Mrs. Kincaid slipped off too.

Marty was late for lunch, but there was such pandemonium in the dining room that nobody noticed. Cheers kept breaking out for the sophomores or the seniors, and Marty practically had to yell to make herself heard. "It's done! Come up and see it after lunch." She plopped a hotdog onto her plate. "Priscilla's almost as pleased with it as I am."

I don't know now whether that was the first time I'd heard Marty call Mrs. Kincaid by her first name, but I do know that by then it seemed perfectly natural.

While we were in the studio and Marty was explaining her

new painting, a huge abstract in primary colors, which I had liked immediately without knowing quite why, cheers from the parking lot announced the arrival of the Southport buses.

"Damn!" she said. "Now we have to go down and be nice little Turnbull dates."

I nodded. It would be the third blind date for me that year, and neither of the others had been worth seeing the first time, let alone again. "We're supposed to like it!"

She made a face. "Pimples and dirty jokes. The last creep I had spent the whole evening complaining about the saltpeter in the mashed potatoes. As if I cared about the level of his sexual appetite."

"Maybe their *macho* image needs an explanation for not trying to rape us in the parking lot."

"With all those faculty members everywhere? I wish this school would decide once and for all whether it wants to go back to Emily's time or join the twentieth century and let us make our own choices."

"They're afraid of what those choices would be."

"They might be surprised." Marty sighed. "They believe all those adolescent psychology books that describe us as slavering sex fiends."

I pulled her out of the studio by her elbow. "A proper Turnbull girl, no matter how bright, talented, and religious, must attend to her social education."

"Well, I don't have *time!*"

"Let's go meet the new Prince Charmings."

"Princes Charming," she corrected me as she slammed the studio door behind us.

By the time the starting whistle blew, snow had begun to fall again. My date, a reasonably presentable sophomore, confided in me that he'd just come to Southport and loathed everything about it. "Do you hate blind dates as much as I do?" he asked, then seemed to hear how the question might have sounded. "I don't mean you, I mean—"

"That's okay. I hate them, too. You're my third this year."

He grinned, and his face, round and freckled and pink-cheeked under reddish brown hair, was friendly.

I grinned too. "I'm afraid I don't remember what they said your name was."

"Chuck."

"Michelle."

"Hi," he said, and tucked the blanket he'd brought more tightly around our legs. I decided that things might just be looking up.

After the first few plays he pulled a pair of heavy glasses out of his pocket. "They told me not to wear these for two reasons. One, that my date might be someone I wanted to impress with my phenomenal good looks and the other, that I might rather not see her. But whichever, I want to see the game." He settled his glasses and turned to look at me. "Not bad," he observed, grinning again.

"Not bad yourself," I replied.

He pushed at a lock of hair on his forehead, a gesture he made every few minutes, though the hair didn't seem long enough to be bothersome. "Oh, that," he said later, when he caught me watching him. "I told you I just came to Southport. They cut my hair, but I can't get over the habit. I used to wear it long to drive my dad crazy."

"Did it work?"

"Too well! I'm here—a pacifist at a military academy."

"There isn't a war now."

"No, but if Southport has anything to do with it, there *will* be."

The snow had begun to fall harder, and was clinging to the grass of the hockey field. "Decent athletes," Chuck observed as Willie kicked the senior wing's goal away at the last split second. "Indecent cheerleaders, though."

He was looking at Bits, who was leading the others in one of their more elaborate routines, with plenty of high kicks. She had them as close to the officials' table as she dared, and I saw that Mr. Kincaid was not concentrating on the game as closely as he might have been. I glanced around to see where Mrs. Kincaid was and spotted her in the top row of bleachers. She, too, was watching the cheerleaders. Her mouth was set in that grim line again, until she chanced to look away and saw me. She grinned then, and waved, so I waved back, then saw Marty in the row beneath, next to a tall, gangly character with an advanced case of acne. She scowled, shielding a thumbs-down sign with one mitten, then pulled the fur collar of her coat up around her face. I looked back at the field as a shout went up around me, and realized that I'd missed the sophomores' first goal. The score was tied 1–1, and the cheerleaders were at it harder than ever.

The snow kept falling as the game went on, and finally the grass disappeared entirely under the coating of white. The players' footprints were being filled in almost as fast as they were made.

"Maybe they'll cancel at the half," Chuck said, scanning the sky. "It doesn't look like stopping."

"They won't cancel this game for anything less than a blizzard," I explained. "It's the game of the season."

Sure enough, when the whistle blew for the half, Mr. Kincaid announced through the bullhorn that the game would continue as long as the teams felt they could see the ball. Both teams called to go on, the spectators joined them, and the second half began on schedule with the score still tied.

Halfway through the third quarter Scovie made a goal and the sophomores went wild. Chuck, who had inhaled some of our enthusiasm, jumped up and down with me. "It'll drive the seniors wild," he warned. "Just watch them now!"

He was right. The senior line took the ball after the bully and started down the field, passing it neatly back and forth, moving fast. Willie grabbed her hockey stick more tightly, and Jeannie, watching the senior inner who had the ball, ran toward her, determined to stop her before she could get inside the striking circle. Just as they came together, Jeannie's foot slipped on the snow and she went down, twisting her leg as she fell. The ball was passed to the center, who made the goal as the whistle sounded to stop the play. Jeannie lay where she had fallen.

Mr. Kincaid jumped up from the table and ran out onto the field, but the players ran over and circled Jeannie, and I couldn't see anything except their backs. Finally, the players moved back, and Mr. Kincaid carried Jeannie awkwardly off the field toward his car. Bits followed them, her orange sweater bright through the falling snow.

Miss Holcomb, the gym coach, explained through the bullhorn that Jeannie would be taken to the hospital for X rays, and the game would be called because of the snow. The last senior goal, having been made as the whistle blew, would not count. The sophomores were declared school champions.

At that, the field dissolved into chaos, seniors booing and demanding a final period of play, sophomores cheering, and everyone climbing down from the bleachers and onto the field.

As the noise level rose, Stoney stood up in the front row, took the bullhorn, and demanded silence. "Hot cider and doughnuts are being served in the dining room. A movie will be shown in the auditorium before dinner."

"I hope it's a good one," Chuck said as we headed for the dining room. "All Southport ever gets are the dregs."

Tag found me at the doughnut table and pulled me away from Chuck. "Have you seen Bits?"

"Not since Mr. Kincaid carried Jeannie off the field."

"Neither has anyone else. Dan's having a fit."

"She probably went with them to the hospital."

"Obviously." Tag frowned. "But she didn't tell anyone. Not Mrs. Kincaid. And not Dan."

"But if she's with Mr. Kincaid, she wouldn't have had to get permission from anybody else, would she? And Jeannie *is* her roommate."

"I know. But do you really think anyone believes that Bits— of all people—would put her roommate before a guy? Particularly a guy she's almost pinned to. Dan is really furious."

I remembered the way Mrs. Kincaid had been looking at the cheerleaders, how close they'd been to the officials' table. But Bits was still just a fifteen-year-old with a crush. "Dan's just being melodramatic," I said. "Besides, they'll probably be back any minute."

"I hope so." Tag went back to her date, but clearly she was worried.

When I joined Chuck, he raised his eyebrows but didn't say anything.

"Just a little class problem," I muttered, taking the cider he was holding out.

"I heard Dan Peterson out in the hall," he said. "Don't worry about it. That guy has an ego like Everest, and your cheerleader friend has been stepping all over it. That didn't start today."

"I thought you were new to Southport."

"Don't let anybody tell you that girls are the only gossips."

By the time we were seated for dinner, Bits still hadn't appeared. Jeannie's date, a friend of Dan's, sat with him and kept him quiet, but it was clear that he was raging.

After dinner, Marty joined me in the bathroom. "Priscilla got a call from Donald," she said, running a comb through her curls. "Jeannie tore the cartilage in her knee, and they're going to operate tomorrow morning." She ran a gloss stick, her only concession to the cosmetic industry, over her lips. "Bits is at the hospital."

"So everybody figured. She'd better get back soon, or Dan's going to go to Stoney and start on her about Mr. Kincaid."

"No problem. Priscilla told Stoney that she suggested Bits stay with Jeannie till she goes to sleep. She's had a sedative, so that won't be long."

I looked at her. "What does Priscilla think?"

Marty fluffed her hair with her fingers. "That Bits is concerned about her roommate's welfare." She turned away from the mirror. "Come on. I don't want to keep the Acne Kid waiting."

"Never judge a book by its cover."

"Oh? Well, this 'book' says he's got dope in the bus and asked me to go out for a smoke during the break. God's out to get me."

"So hook up your direct line tomorrow and bawl Him out."

We met our dates at the gym door. "Who's the classy one?" Chuck asked, as Marty and her date went into the gym ahead of us.

"My roommate," I answered, feeling unaccountably proud of her.

"She's too good for that peasant she's with!" He swiped at the hair on his forehead. "A genuine princess."

I didn't bother to explain why I laughed.

When Bits finally got back, there was less than an hour left of the dance. She appeared in the gym, still dressed in her cheerleading outfit.

But before Bits found Dan, Stoney put a hand on her shoulder. "I'm sure Mr. Peterson will excuse you while you change into something more appropriate for a dance. He'll expect you to be back in a few minutes!"

"This place is more like Southport than I thought," Chuck whispered. "That lady would make a great commandant."

"How true."

When the last dance was over, Chuck put his coat around my shoulders and took my hand as we walked through the snow to the bus. "I've had a better time than I expected," he said, pushing at his hair.

"Me too."

"No more blind dates?"

"Okay."

"I'll invite you to our dances, you invite me to yours, and we'll bask in the glow of this mad love affair for the rest of the year." He kissed my cheek. "I might survive after all." He took his coat, jumped onto the step of the bus and waved. *"Pax vobiscum!"*

As I hurried, shivering, back inside, I passed Bits and Dan, twined around each other in the shadow of a bush. "I guess they got it solved," I thought.

Scovie caught up with me as I opened the door into the dorm. "Did you see Bits and Dan out there? Pure show! Even Bits knows she goofed this time."

The Kincaids were standing outside their apartment door, their arms around each other's waists, wishing everyone good night. I was reminded of Bits and Dan in the shadows. Certainly everything *looked* okay.

When Bits came up, she passed the Kincaids without a word, and a few minutes later they went into their apartment. Usually after a dance it takes at least an hour for the dorm to settle down for the night. That night everyone was unusually quiet.

When Marty got into bed, she groaned. "Well, another dance survived. And another blind date bites the dust!"

I thought about Chuck and smiled. "I think I found a friend."

"Bully!" Marty turned over and pulled the blankets around her shoulders.

She wasn't ever particularly cheerful after a dance, but I wondered if some of her reaction had to do with Bits and Mr. Kincaid. And I wondered how Mrs. Kincaid really felt. "Bits is only fifteen," I thought for the umpteenth time that day. And then I thought about Chuck pushing at that imaginary lock of hair and decided that I didn't care about Bits one way or another.

❧ S E V E N ❧

That night I had one of my stranger dreams. Dad was in it, and Georgie. It must have been years since I'd dreamed about them. Georgie was playing with some trucks outside the door of my bedroom at home, making *vroom vroom* sounds at the top of his lungs, and I was trying to get my doll to go to sleep. I yelled at Georgie to shut up and started out into the hall. But when I opened the door, it wasn't the hall at home anymore, it was Miss Engles' apartment. And I wasn't me anymore either; I was Miss Engles. At least I think I was. The apartment was mine, anyway. And Dad was there, sitting in the leather chair. I started to go over to him and then he wasn't there anymore, Chuck was. Only he was making the *vroom vroom* sounds. It was as if he were reading them off a paper he was holding, and I knew that the paper was a poem of mine. I took it away from him so I could read it right, but I couldn't read it with my eyes closed, so I opened them. And there I was in my bed at Turnbull, awake.

It was such a weird dream that I couldn't tell how I felt about it—I just knew that it didn't seem to want to let go of me. Maybe it was the leftover feeling from the dream that made everything feel wrong around the dorm that morning. Or maybe I just had my antennae out, and they were picking up on what was really there.

The Kincaids weren't at breakfast or chapel, but they seldom went to chapel anyway. When they didn't show up for dinner, Marty dismissed it.

"They probably wanted to eat at home for a change," she said. "They do have a kitchen, you know."

But I noticed that a couple of times she went to their door and then left without knocking. I didn't think it was only their privacy she was thinking of.

In the hour before I had to be at the Penwomen meeting, I climbed onto the breakwater. I don't know why I went there. It was cold, and the waves kept throwing up a fine icy spray. Even through my boots and wool socks I could feel the cold of the limestone. I knew there would soon be a coating of ice that would keep us off the breakwater until spring. Maybe it was just a kind of farewell to the place where I could be completely out of sight of the campus and the buildings, just me and Lake Huron.

I didn't feel depressed, exactly, just sort of stopped. It was as if I'd gotten stranded somewhere between Chuck and Marty and the D.E.T.s, between Miss Engles and the Kincaids, between Turnbull and home, when I was little and we were a family. I felt as if I were floating, as if I'd gotten detached from who I was. I looked at my hands in their heavy red and white mittens, and it was like they belonged to someone else. I looked down at my feet, and they seemed too far away from my face, as if I'd grown too tall. How could the skin that covered me when I was six have stretched to cover all this body?

When it was time to go to Miss Engles', I went, but I still felt strange, and the feeling that my feet shouldn't be so far away stuck with me as I climbed the stairs that led to her apartment on the third floor. Those funny big mittened hands knocked, and it was almost a surprise when Jenny Brown, the president of Penwomen, opened the door. I wouldn't have been surprised if, just like in my dream, the door and stairs had just melted away and I'd found myself already inside. The leather chair was already taken, of course, and I ended up on the floor by the window. I sat there thinking how perfectly my dream had reproduced the room with its slanted ceilings and dormers, the white walls with the bright abstract paintings, the hanging plants, and the endless bookcases. But there wasn't any sense now that it was mine.

The discussion that day was about a short story one of the seniors had written. All I can remember about that story is that I thought it was awful. The discussion must have been lively, but I couldn't keep my mind on it. I found myself looking at the paintings and wondering about the stories that went around about Miss Engles and the artist. They were all by the same person, whose last name was scrawled illegibly across the lower right corners. Word was that there had been a tragic love affair. Some said it ended in suicide, that the artist had been an alcoholic; others said that he had jilted her to run off with another woman. No one seemed able to believe that a middle-aged woman could actually have chosen not to marry, or that she might have several paintings by one person without having had an affair with him. But then if you were to believe all the stories about the faculty, you'd think no one came to teach at Turnbull without a tragedy in her background.

I had just decided that Miss Engles probably hadn't even met the artist, but had bought the paintings at a gallery, when I was handed a cup of cocoa and realized the discussion was over. As people began to put on their coats, Miss Engles asked if I would stay and help her clean up. Usually she asked one of the seniors. I thought about going back to the dorm and about how comfortable it seemed here, and nodded.

"Anything you want to talk about?" she asked when she was washing the cocoa cups and I was drying them. "You haven't said a word since you got here."

How could I tell her what was bothering me, when it was all so vague? Did other people suddenly feel they'd come unglued from their hands and feet? Or that they were in danger of turning into someone else? "It's nothing," I said.

"When you sit through a discussion like that without saying anything at all, *something's* wrong."

I put the cup carefully on the counter and reached for another. It was one thing to write down how I felt, another to talk about it. Talk happens too fast. You think of something, but by the time you get the right words, the time is gone, and the person is pushing you on to something else. Everything gets distorted. Miss Engles had stopped washing cups, her hands resting on the edge of the sink. She was watching me with those penetrating eyes. Even without looking at her I felt them. I looked at her hands instead and thought how strong they seemed, how exactly right for her. She could never have looked down at them and thought they should belong to someone else. The silence in the room was stretching too far. One of us would have to say something.

"Did you ever lose your hands?" The moment I said it, I knew why I hated talking. Without all the thinking that led up to it, the question must have sounded insane. I wished I'd gone back to the dorm.

"You'll have to give me some background for that one," she said, and put a cup into the water.

"Have you ever looked at your hands and wondered if they

were really yours? Or your feet—as if you'd grown too tall, too far away from them?"

She rinsed the cup and handed it to me before she spoke. "I remember looking at my hands one day and seeing that they were my mother's hands, with the blue veins standing out on the backs the way they did on my mother's hands when I was little. Maybe it isn't quite the same, but it did feel strange. I think it's a sense of having grown up on the outside without changing inside."

I turned and looked at her directly for the first time. "That's it! That's exactly it, only until you said it, I didn't really know that's what I meant."

"It happens to everybody one way or another. I remember a friend of mine once saying that when he was a little boy his aunts and uncles seemed entirely different from himself. They were 'grown-ups.' Then one day he realized that he was thirty-five, older than his aunts and uncles had been at the time he was remembering. But *he* didn't feel at all 'grown up.' We notice that we change, but it's never how we think it ought to be. It never seems to be 'growing up.' "

I started to laugh, and then, for no reason at all, I was crying. Miss Engles took the towel out of my hand and pushed me toward the living room. She went on doing dishes while I sat in the leather chair and cried. I remembered my dream, and Georgie, and then knew that part of why I was crying was that for Georgie there could never be any growing up, any losing his feet. He would never be anything except a little boy, going *vroom vroom* in the hall. I hadn't cried about him, hadn't even thought about him, for a very long time. And now I couldn't seem to stop.

"I'm sorry," I said, when I could finally talk.

Miss Engles had finished in the kitchen and brought me a Kleenex. "Don't be sorry. We've all got a right to cry when we feel like it. The people I'm sorry for are the ones who never let themselves cry."

"I don't know what that was all about."

"Who says it has to be rational?"

"I'd better be getting back to the dorm." I thought about the Kincaids' closed door and that tension in the dorm and wished I could stay. Then, maybe because I'd been crying, because I'd already been talking about the kinds of things I usually saved for my poetry, I asked a question I hadn't expected to ask. "Do you think it's possible that something is going on between Bits and Mr. Kincaid?"

"Sounds as if you do."

"No. I mean, I don't think I do. But she did go to the hospital with him last night, and they were gone an awfully long time."

"She went to be with her roommate. And her roommate needed someone to stay for a while. But I suspect Bits wasn't thinking only about Jeannie."

"I don't think Mrs. Kincaid likes Bits."

"She probably isn't the only one in school who feels that way. But it doesn't necessarily mean she thinks anything is 'going on,' as you put it. Kids do get crushes."

"Tag's worried, and Tag is usually right."

"Ah, the lure of E.S.P. Mike, I don't know the truth about the situation any more than anyone else. What I do know is that Miss Stonehill took a calculated risk in bringing the Kincaids onto the campus. It's rough enough for one person to have to act as a role model. It's worse for two people to handle that responsibility along with a marriage. Marriage is hard enough without having to feel as if you have to prove the value of the whole institution. If it makes you feel any better, you might think of it this way. If a high school sophomore with a crush really can do damage to a relationship between adults, they already had problems."

I nodded, not sure whether I felt reassured or not.

"Relationships are *never* easy or safe or certain." She grinned. "But except for ourselves, Mike, they're all we've got!"

As I walked back to school, keeping my head down against the wind off the lake, I watched my feet take each step. They were back where they belonged. The detached feeling had gone. "Except for ourselves," she'd said. And I didn't know which was more complicated, myself or other people.

As I went upstairs to the dorm, I saw Bits standing at the landing window, looking out toward the lake. When she heard me behind her, she turned and went past me down the stairs as if she hadn't recognized me. I glanced out the window as I passed and saw Marty and Mrs. Kincaid walking beside the breakwater. It seemed a good thing that the Kincaids weren't locked away in their apartment anymore.

❧ EIGHT ❧

After the night of the Hockey Dance, the atmosphere in the
dorm began to change. The differences were small. Instead of
the Friday night get-togethers in the apartment, there were
gatherings in the lounge. Sometimes Mrs. Kincaid would be
there, and sometimes Mr. Kincaid would be there, but seldom
both. The door to their apartment, which had always been
open, was closed more often than not. The feeling of family began to disappear, and life got more and more the way it was in
the other dorms. Occasionally someone would hear raised
voices coming from behind their closed door, but usually the
tension between them was more subtle, not so much a new dif-
ficulty between them as a sense of something missing. Even
when they were together, they didn't seem as aware of each
other as they had been before.

Gradually, we got used to the change. Or maybe it was that
Christmas came, with the Christmas program and caroling and
parties and extra church services. Then the long vacation, and
after that the tensions of exam week. We were too busy to notice much else.

When first-semester grades came out, I'd managed to get
back my place at the top of the class. Latin was still hard, but

after a year, I was beginning to handle it better. I was even getting vaguely interested in Caesar's campaigns. Still, it was less my interest in Caesar than Marty's in her painting that made the difference. She was spending so much time painting, thinking about painting, and reading about painting that she scarcely had time for anything else, and her grades showed it. Tag, despite her addiction to science-fiction novels, edged Marty out for second place, so she'd slipped from first to third.

"Just barely in the top ten percent of my class," Marty observed. "How will I ever make it into college?"

Scovie and Willie both agreed that there was far too much emphasis on academic competition at Turnbull. Neither seemed concerned about being lost somewhere in the middle of the sophomore class. For Bits, though, grades were no laughing matter. Between cheerleading and her scholarship job, "to say nothing of all the time she spends mooning over Kincaid," Tag pointed out, she'd neglected her classes badly. American history was her only *A*, a fact that didn't do anything to counteract the suspicions—and overall, she'd slipped to a bare *C* average.

"If she doesn't bring her grades up by the end of next semester," Jeannie agonized, "she'll lose her scholarship!"

The Monday after grades came out, as I was on my way to Miss Engles' classroom after school, I found Jeannie and Bits in a library alcove, Jeannie patting ineffectually at Bits' back as Bits cried. Everyone tries not to notice emotional outbursts at that time of year, and the others in the library were carefully ignoring the two of them. When I went to ask if I could do anything to help, Bits pushed Jeannie away and ran into the classroom corridor, past Mr. Kincaid's room, leaving Jeannie looking as miserable as if the grades had been her own. I started into the classroom wing myself and saw Mr. Kincaid come out of his classroom. I pulled back out of sight and watched him hurry off in the direction Bits had gone. When I went to find Miss Engles, they were nowhere to be seen.

❦ ❦

Late in January, I had a nasty encounter with my deeper self. Marty found out about a contest she seemed sure to win, and I came up against a feeling I didn't like. Maybe it had been getting back first place in class—I didn't much think about the fact that Marty could have been first if she'd been working— but I wasn't sure I wanted to see the Princess add another jewel to her crown.

St. Mark's Cathedral in Detroit was redesigning its main sanctuary and had asked Episcopal high school students all over the state to submit designs for a stained-glass window. The winner's window was to be used in the sanctuary, and there was a five-hundred-dollar prize as well. Between Marty's talent and her religion, I didn't see how she could miss. I didn't like the feeling of competition, the tiny nagging hope that she might lose. Was she my best friend or not? How would her winning hurt me? But I couldn't quite get rid of that tiny hope.

A few days later, Marty came into the room, waving her sketchbook over her head. "I've had the most phenomenal idea! I'm going to do the Stations of the Cross!"

I put my biology book down. It didn't seem to be the time to learn the life cycle of mosses. "I assume you're talking about that contest."

She opened her sketchbook and dropped it on the desk in front of me. "Remember the sketches from the chapel I did last fall? I was looking through them, trying to get an idea, when I came across the Stations of the Cross. It's perfect!"

One has to be patient with genius. "*What* is?"

Marty looked as if she were dealing with an idiot. "The idea. To do the Stations of the Cross." She flipped pages in her sketchbook, and I got only vague impressions of her sketches as they flew by.

"All fourteen of them? On one window?"

"No. One window for each one! You see, I enter just one, and if it wins the contest, maybe they'll want all the others. Every church has to have the Stations somewhere. And when they ask, lo and behold, I'll have the others ready—presto! Fourteen windows sold!"

"So much for humility." I looked up from the sketchbook into her face. The pink glow was in her cheeks again, that brightness in her eyes. "You're mad!"

"Of course. Artists are—by definition. And so are poets. That's the reason we can stand each other."

She began to describe her idea, and I began to catch her excitement. She'd been working on abstract painting with Mrs. Kincaid all year, and now she wanted to try some of the same techniques with her window designs. The Stations of the Cross in the Turnbull chapel were old-fashioned and representational, and she wanted to try to catch the feelings of each one without the pictures.

The contest deadline was March 31, and Marty threw herself into the work of designing the windows to the exclusion of almost everything else. She began going to early Mass every morning "to absorb the atmosphere," and staying up far past lights out. It got so that I hardly saw her at all. If she wasn't in class, she was either in the chapel or the studio. She skipped gym and spent study halls in the studio till she got a warning from Stoney herself. But even then there wasn't time for homework. Even in Latin she started failing quizzes, gave up answering questions in class, and never had her translations finished. I tried to get her to sleep some, before she ended up sick, but she wouldn't listen. She would do a design ten ways, then tear it up and start again.

Finally, I persuaded Miss Engles to go with me to talk to her. Mrs. Kincaid was so involved with the window designs herself that she didn't see what they were doing to the rest of Marty's life. We went up to the studio one afternoon and found Marty sitting on a stool, bent over the design table. She looked up in surprise as we walked in, the shadows under her eyes looking even more pronounced in the light from the work lamp.

"May I see the famous sketches?" Miss Engles asked. "Mike tells me they're almost as good as her poetry."

It was the first time Miss Engles had seen any of Marty's recent work, and as she looked at one after another of the rough sketches, she smiled in a way I always hoped she'd smile when I took her something I'd written. It was a smile I didn't often get.

"These are fine," she said quietly, and I thought how powerful a word that could be when it was said that way. "When is the deadline?"

Marty ran a hand through her hair. She was more exhausted and discouraged than she'd admit. "The end of the month."

"I imagine you're ready to decide which one to submit, so there will be time to get it finished. Ten days should give you time to get one of them just the way you want it."

Marty looked at the sketches as if she'd never seen them before. "I've been so involved in the whole set, I'd actually forgotten that only one had to be done by the deadline. How dumb!"

"Not so dumb," Miss Engles said with a smile. "They're a

set, so they had to be designed together. It's just that now you can finish one, and if St. Mark's gives you reason to finish the others, you can do those. If they don't, you've got a fine series of sketches!"

Marty frowned. "How am I going to choose which one?"

"Maybe Mrs. Kincaid can help. Meanwhile"—the gray eyes snapped—"if you don't have your *Julius Caesar* paper in by Wednesday, you'll be dangerously close to a mid-semester *C* in English!"

Marty grinned at me. "Render unto Caesar . . ."

I laughed. "And Shakespeare, and Engles!"

As Miss Engles and I left, I had another confrontation with myself. I'd asked Miss Engles to talk to Marty, but it was hard to accept her reaction to Marty's work. I couldn't decide whether I'd somehow expected her not to like it or whether I thought she'd automatically appreciate it less than my poetry or what. I spent the rest of the afternoon brooding in my room, remembering Cassius' lines from *Julius Caesar*: "The fault, dear Brutus, is not in our stars, / But in ourselves, that we are underlings."

In the next week, once Marty'd decided which design to finish, she settled back into her old routine, with time for sleep and studying as well as work. By the time the deadline came and her design was safely in the mail, she had almost caught up with her classes. We settled in to wait.

She was waiting to hear about the contest, but I was waiting for spring. Once April arrives, I always expect to wake up and find the snow gone, the grass miraculously green. And of course it doesn't happen. Classes dragged; I didn't feel like writing anything except my journal, and that from force of habit. Miss Engles and I suspended our Monday afternoon meetings, since I wasn't writing anything for her to look at.

Even Scovie and Willie were affected. The snow had lost its joy, the snowball fights and tobogganing trips ended, the ice-skating rink alternately thawed and froze, becoming bumpy and impossible. Scovie tried for a while to drum up interest in a class volleyball team, but there wasn't enough energy in the whole class to field a single team. Chuck and I wrote a few let-ters, but there didn't seem to be much to say. Southport was in the same winter doldrums.

After Easter vacation it was worse. The days inched by, gray and cold and wet. Ice chunks bumped against the breakwater, blending with the pale sky, looking as if they'd never melt. Tensions mounted for everybody. The Kincaids seemed to be together less than ever, and when they were, there was a si-lence between them like a wall.

Then one Saturday morning Marty woke me early. When I opened my eyes, ready to yell about the hour, I saw a shaft of sunlight falling across the quilt on her bed. The window was open and a breeze stirred the curtains, bringing with it the heavy, green smell of spring.

"Let's go for a walk," Marty said.

I got dressed quickly, and we slipped out, avoiding the lounge, where a few early risers were already at the doughnuts. The last vestiges of snow were gone; the ground was wet and puddling, green beginning to color the grass. We picked our way among the puddles and walked along the breakwater until we came to the iron fence that marked the north end of the campus. It was as far as we could get from the buildings. We climbed up the limestone blocks, down the other side, and stood looking at the deep green of the lake swirling around the rocks with each slow surge of wave.

Marty took a deep breath, then another. "Dark and light," she said. "Lent and Easter."

I watched a seagull circle lazily over our heads, its wings glinting silver against the fresh blue of the sky, and added my own pair to the pattern. "Winter and spring." The seagull suddenly plunged downward, moving its wings at the last moment, almost brushing the water, and climbed again. I looked at Marty. "Are we playing opposites?"

"No. I was just thinking about beginnings. I'm going to win that contest."

She said it with such calm conviction it was as if she'd read it in a newspaper. "It's a beginning for me. I know it just as surely as you know spring has to get here eventually. It's all just a matter of patience. When I opened my eyes to that sunlight this morning, I knew."

"I don't think I can stand another Tag." I kicked at a pool of rainwater in a hollow of rock. "How can anybody know anything as certainly as that before it happens?"

Marty shrugged. "It's never happened to me before, but for some reason I trust it. I'll win the contest and that'll be the beginning of the end of Jane's getting her way with Dad about me. They won't be able to stop what's going to happen any more than they could stop a season." Marty's face was calm, but her eyes looked troubled.

"If you're so sure about all this, why aren't you jumping and shouting?" I asked. "You don't even look really happy."

She looked away, back over the breakwater toward the buildings, tinged yellow with the early sun. "Because there's something else—a shadow or something. You don't get spring without winter first. You can't have Easter without Lent. I can't shake the feeling that it's happening the wrong way round. That something dark is out there too."

"It's superstition," I said. "The evil eye! Lots of people

think they have to pay for anything good that happens to them."

"I know, but this is more than that. I can't figure out what it is exactly, but it's as certain as the feeling that I'm going to win that contest."

Another seagull had joined the first, and they swooped in lazy circles, almost as if they were playing.

"There," I said. "Watch the seagulls. They know better than to worry about darkness when the sun's out. It's spring!" As soon as I'd said it, the craziness that happens to me in the spring took hold. I jumped up onto the rock above me and from there to the next, breathing the warm, soft air in great gulps. "Race you to the swings!" I called, and ran off toward the old playground equipment standing in its weeds and rust a hundred yards farther down the iron fence.

Marty followed and we spent the next hour swinging, jouncing each other on the teeter-totter, climbing the jungle gym. That morning, the first true day of spring, we might have been five years old. That morning Eden was as real as it had ever been, and the sky above it was clean and blue and sunny.

❦ NINE ❦

Once Marty had decided she was going to win the contest, everything began to happen very fast. I was on my way to history class on Monday when she grabbed my arm and pulled me out of the hall traffic into an empty classroom. Her face was white, almost grim, but her eyes were sparkling. She put a letter into my hand. "Read it. Tell me what it says."

I scanned it as quickly as I could. It congratulated Marty on winning the contest and said that the review board was interested in seeing the sketches for the other Stations of the Cross. It suggested a meeting in Detroit the following weekend.

I threw my arms around her—it was like hugging a tree. Pushing her away, I looked at her hard. "Do you mean you haven't read it yet?"

"I've read it. Three times. I just wanted you to tell me I'm not having a dream. They want to see the sketches, don't they?"

"And meet you. That crazy idea of yours is actually working!" The final bell rang for class. "We're late. Where are your books?"

Marty shook her head. "I guess I left them upstairs. Tell Kincaid I'll be there in a minute." She took the letter back and ran down the hall.

"Miss Sheffield needn't come to class at all if she doesn't care to be here when we're ready to begin," Mr. Kincaid said when I explained that Marty was on her way. He closed the classroom door. "A rule is a rule."

I caught Scovie's eye as I slipped into my seat, and she shrugged. Bits, in her front-row seat by the window, was smiling. I knew what she'd say when she found out Marty had won five hundred dollars. She wouldn't think about the honor or about the art at all. It would just be the Princess getting richer.

As it turned out, Marty didn't even try to come to class. She and Priscilla went to Stoney's office to tell her the news and get permission to go to Detroit the next weekend. They would stay over for church on Sunday so that Marty could see the cathedral during a service.

The announcement was made in the dining room at dinner, and it was as if the whole student body was seeing Marty for the first time. Seniors who never bothered to notice a sophomore's existence would stop her in the hall and congratulate her. Other art students asked Mrs. Kincaid to put up a display of Marty's work. But the change that shook me most was in the D.E.T.s. Scovie and Willie, whose respect for Marty's athletic skill had soured when she quit sports to concentrate on her painting, were suddenly friendly. They took to dropping in after softball to tell Marty how practice had gone. Jeannie actually brought both of us cookies from her mother's latest Care package. I felt a little like a puppy, hanging around the table to pick up the crumbs. Tag was, as usual, quiet. But in that quiet was a new quality of approval, of admiration. It made me wonder about success.

I wondered if the D.E.T.s were able to accept Marty's talent in art because it didn't threaten them. None of the others had any desire to be known as an artist, and so they weren't being shown up. And since everybody in the school was being so impressed, some of the glory might rub off a little on whoever was seen to be one of Marty's friends. It wasn't that I thought anyone was actually thinking any of those things. It was just so unreal to see the D.E.T.s treating Marty as one of us.

Bits, of course, was the exception. If anything, the change in the others pushed her away even farther. The change in Jeannie was especially hard for Bits to take. No matter how anyone else ever treated Bits, Jeannie was always the adoring roommate. Bits, who found it so hard to accept Marty's wealth, had at least had the D.E.T.s to hold up to her. Rich or not, Marty didn't belong at Turnbull the way Bits did. Now even that seemed to be disintegrating, and Bits began to be downright nasty.

"It's weird," I told Marty one evening after Bits had made some snide remark as she'd passed us on the stairs, "but I actually think I prefer the way Bits is taking all this to the way the rest of them are."

"Why?"

"Because at least it seems more honest. She's got the same old reasons for disliking you—but the others have changed completely, just because you won a contest. *You* haven't changed."

Marty glanced at herself in the mirror and made a face. "You mean the sudden blossoming of my genius hasn't shown up on the outside?"

"Sorry. Just the same old face." I thought about how I'd felt when she first told me about the contest. At least I hadn't been as jealous when she won as I'd thought I'd be. "Still, doesn't it sort of scare you that people want to be friends just because of a little success?"

"No," Marty said, and I could see she meant it. "I'm me. And whether they see me as Princess or Artist or whatever, it can't change who I am. Or what I can do. I'm the only one I have to please. And maybe Priscilla, a little."

Despite Marty's reaction, it bothered me a lot.

Saturday morning, before Priscilla and Marty were to leave, the class threw a party in the lounge. Instead of the usual dough-nuts and sweet rolls, there was a huge sheet cake with the words *Fame* and *Fortune* in red frosting above the outline of a church. "Such taste!" she whispered in my ear when she saw it. But she smiled graciously and accepted the honor as if she were used to having the whole class at her feet. I decided grow-ing up in the world of the Sheffields had a few advantages.

Donald Kincaid was there, one of the few times the Kincaids had attended a class gathering together in weeks. It was a clear show of houseparently solidarity, the sharing of a family mem-ber's success. The only one who wasn't there was Bits, her ab-sence made more noticeable by Jeannie's overwhelming presence. She cut the cake, bustled about handing it out, and made a long speech of praise in her best, most flowery prose.

There was no clue to how nervous Marty was until I caught a look of such desperation that I grabbed her by the sleeve of her robe and pulled her to the door of the lounge. "The Princess has to get dressed," I said. "Enjoy the cake!"

"Thank you all for this," Marty said in the doorway. "You don't know what it means to me."

In our room I was finally able to laugh. "You don't know what it means to me," I repeated. "And a damn good thing, too!"

"I don't know what you mean," Marty said innocently. "Such a lovely cake! Such noble sentiments!" She sank onto her bed. "Cake for breakfast. *Yuck!*"

When Mrs. Kincaid appeared at our door, Marty was staring into her closet as if she were surveying a rack of particularly depressing Salvation Army castoffs. "Priscilla, help!" she wailed. "I don't know what to wear!"

"Don't worry about clothes," she said. "There's not a thing in that closet that wouldn't be fine. They're church people, you know. Anything a Sheffield wears ought to fit right in. I'm the one who'll scare them."

She was right. I looked at her velvet pants tucked into boots, her beads and feathers. Whatever Marty chose, she'd look safe by comparison.

"Anyway," Mrs. Kincaid went on, "it isn't your clothes they're interested in, it's those windows."

With Mrs. Kincaid to help, Marty was soon dressed, her suitcase packed, her portfolio filled. "Take your charcoals," Mrs. Kincaid said. "I'll take you to a gallery or two where I know some people who'd like to see them."

And then it was time to go. I took Marty's suitcase, and the three of us went down the back way to avoid being seen. Marty didn't want any more fuss. Over her cheekbones and nose the skin looked pulled tight; on the hand that held her portfolio the knuckles were white spots.

The day was warm, the breeze soft. It was the kind of day that made me think of roller skating. A robin hopped through the grass near the parking lot, its head tilted to one side.

"An omen," Priscilla said, as she settled Marty's portfolio and suitcase in the back of the battered Volvo. "He came to wish you luck."

"New life," Marty said.

The bird jabbed the ground and came up with a worm wiggling vainly in its beak. "For the bird at least," I thought, and wondered if Marty's fears were rubbing off on me.

"My suitcase!" Priscilla yelped as she was about to slam the trunk. "I left it in the apartment when I came to help you pack and forgot to go back for it."

"I'll get it," I offered.

Marty grabbed my hand. "We'll both go. Then you can stay upstairs. I don't think I want you standing in the driveway when we leave. I just want to sneak away."

Priscilla started the car as we ran for the building.

When we reached the door to the dorm, laughing and panting, Marty stopped. She squeezed my hand. "Wish me luck. Next time you see me it'll all have started."

I hugged her. "Today for you, some other day for me."

She opened the door and pushed me through. "You can't help it if you're a late bloomer!"

I stuck out my tongue and started down the hall toward our room, tears prickling in my eyes. Marty went into the Kincaids' apartment.

Halfway down the hall I heard the apartment door slam and turned around. Bits, her face scarlet, ran toward her room. I stood still, biting my lip. A moment later, Marty came out with Priscilla's suitcase, her face as red as Bits'. She didn't look my way, just ducked out of the dorm and down the stairs. I stepped into the doorway of the nearest room and waited.

When the apartment door opened again, I knew what I'd been waiting for. Donald Kincaid stepped into the hall and looked toward the door Marty had just gone through, then the other way, towards Bits' and Jeannie's room. He ran the back of his hand over his mouth a few times, then took a step in the direction Bits had gone. He hesitated, took another step, then turned and went back to the apartment, closing the door firmly behind him.

I had thought I'd go to our window and watch Marty and Priscilla leave. Now I just stood where I was, surprised at the taste of blood in my mouth where I'd bitten right through my lip. Over and over in my mind I saw the robin, that comforting, joyful sign of spring, with a worm wriggling in its beak. Wasn't anything just undiluted good?

The party in the lounge was breaking up. I went back to the room, stuck a Kleenex on my lip, and sat down at my desk. Out of habit, I opened my journal, then just sat there, staring at the empty pages.

There was a knock at the door, then Scovie was beside me, a piece of cake in her hand. "Brought you some cake! You didn't eat a thing in there. And then we're going roller skating. It's a *glorious* day!" She looked at the Kleenex in my hand, then at my lip, which was feeling puffy. "Somebody slug you?"

"I bit my lip."

Willie came in, a pair of old metal skates around her neck. "Let's get this show on the road." She looked at my lip too. "What's going on around here? Bits is having hysterics, Jeannie refuses to leave her alone, and you look like somebody's been beating on you."

"It's nothing."

"Some nothing." I hadn't noticed Tag standing quietly in the doorway. She frowned, her dark eyebrows nearly meeting. "Kincaid sure left the party early. Emily Turnbull knew more about men than anyone gives her credit for."

"Screw Emily Turnbull!" Scovie said. "Whatever she knew, she's dead, remember? Anyway, Bits and Kincaid are nobody's business but their own."

I looked at my journal, its empty pages staring blankly back at me, and decided to go skating with them.

Willie clomped off down the hall singing, "Spring has sprung, the grass has riz, I wonder where the birdies is."

Scovie shrugged and followed, then Tag, shaking her head.

As I closed the door of our room, I thought about the robin and the worm and wondered which was the real symbol of spring. Dark and light, Marty had said. Dark and light.

❧ TEN ❧

I watched Donald Kincaid and Bits all that weekend, not really knowing what I expected to see. There was nothing. Mr. Kincaid's eyes were closed off, perhaps more than ever. Bits spent most of her time in her room with Jeannie.

Late Sunday afternoon, when Marty and Mrs. Kincaid got back, Mr. Kincaid went out to meet them in the parking lot, offering to help with suitcases, all hugging and congratulations. Marty avoided him. If she could have avoided even shaking hands with him, she would have. Back in our room, she didn't mention Saturday morning.

"They're going to take all fourteen," she said, and her voice was a strange blend of excitement and something else, as if she wanted both to shout and to swallow the words back down.

"It was almost like magic, the way it worked," she said, standing at the window and looking out over the campus. "The whole point of their remodeling is to try for a blend of the traditional and the contemporary. My windows fit into their concept so well it was as if it had all been planned."

"It's that direct line to God," I said. "Maybe you didn't do those designs at all."

"Don't laugh," she said, laughing herself. "Sometimes it is

like that. I can try and try and try to get a design right, and nothing works. Then I quit in a fury and later—there it is. Like a door opened while I wasn't looking, and the whole thing popped through. All I have to do is put it down."

"I know. It's like that with poetry. Sometimes the harder I try the farther I get from what I want. Like one time when we were on the breakwater and you were sketching. I looked at the lake and I looked at the sketch and all of a sudden something came into my mind that wanted to be a poem. Except that it didn't come with words. Just a feeling I couldn't seem to catch. I watched you for a while and your hands seemed so sure, everything they did gave that sketch more life. I was crazy with envy right then. And I couldn't figure out how I could even have an idea for a poem without at least some words to go with it. How do we think without words? The next day during biology class, suddenly the words were there."

"What I don't understand," she said, "is how you can go through that process and not believe in God. . . ."

"I never said I didn't. Only that I don't know."

"Such a coward," Marty said.

"Anyway, I believe in something. Call it whatever you want."

"What I believe in now is work! I've got thirteen window designs to finish before the end of school. Less than six weeks to go!"

There wasn't much time for the news of Marty's success with the St. Mark's board to remain the major topic of conversation at Turnbull. The next Saturday was the Spring Ball, the final and biggest social event of the year. Traditionally, the Spring

Ball is a time for pinnings, for the occasional engagement announcement by a senior (though the faculty frowns on that kind
of commitment). There are no blind dates for the ball, and it's
as close as Turnbull gets to a prom, lasting two hours later than
any other dance and including a full-scale banquet beforehand.
Anyone who doesn't have a date from town or a Southport cadet for the Spring Ball doesn't go, and naturally looks like a social failure.

I was safe, of course, with Chuck. We'd seen each other several times since the Hockey Dance and we'd become good
friends. It wasn't very romantic, but it was fun. Scovie and Willie had found Southport boys, Bits would be with Dan, and
Jeannie with one of Dan's friends as usual. Jeannie's dates
changed from one dance to the next, but she was sure to have
one. Tag had invited one of the acolytes.

Marty refused to go. She hadn't met a blind date she could
tolerate and refused to invite any of them. When I assured her
that any one of them would be happy to be her date, she just
laughed. "Of course. Why wouldn't a frog want to dance with a
princess?" But I couldn't persuade her to invite someone just
to keep from looking bad.

"It's only a few hours! Couldn't you put up with one of them
for that long?"

"Why should I? Anybody who really wants to go could get a
date, and everybody knows it. And even if they do think I
couldn't find anyone, what difference would it make? I'm the
famous artist now. Let them just think artists are weird. They
do anyway, you know."

I couldn't understand Marty's self-confidence any more than
I ever had. Nobody else was so unconcerned about what other
people would think. Finally, I put it down to being raised a

Sheffield. Or maybe it was genetic. If I were going to go on writing poetry, I thought, I should get that way myself. But I knew it wouldn't happen.

As the day of the ball drew closer, the level of excitement in the dorm rose steadily. Dresses were taken out and pressed, trips to hairdressers were arranged, and the tension between the Kincaids became more and more noticeable. Usually the dorm mother would be right in the middle of the dance preparations, altering dresses, making suggestions, generally fussing over everyone. The Kincaids all but disappeared behind their door, showing up in the dorm only as often as necessary to keep some sort of order. The possibility of divorce began to be whispered about, throwing shadows over all the preparations for the dance. Marty appeared to ignore the talk, keeping to herself with her work on the other windows.

But it was not the Kincaids who bothered me so much, it was Bits. Less than an hour after Priscilla and Marty had come back from Detroit, Priscilla had called Bits in and told her she would no longer be needed to clean the apartment. Considering that Bits was losing not only her excuse to be near Donald but also her source of pocket money, she took it very well. At least that's the way it looked. But there was a change. Bits had always griped and complained about plenty of things, but she'd had her enthusiasms, too—cheerleaders, her clothes designs. Now she was withdrawn. Apparently she was working on her dress for the Spring Ball, but she wasn't talking about it to anyone; she wasn't showing it off and asking for compliments. She didn't seem to be talking to anyone except Jeannie. And if she had to be anywhere that Marty was, she shut up inside herself completely. If she saw Marty coming toward her in the hall, she'd suddenly find a reason to turn around and go the other way. By the end of the week, Jeannie was doing the same thing. Since everyone else was still treating Marty as the great artist, their behavior was particularly noticeable.

"What did you do to her?" Scovie asked finally. "Steal her false eyelashes?"

Marty just shrugged.

I told myself that whatever might have been happening between Bits and Mr. Kincaid, it had ended and that Bits was bound to get over it eventually, but I couldn't help being uneasy. Tag, as usual, wasn't talking, but seemed to be watching Bits too. She wasn't any happier about the way Bits was acting than I was.

When Saturday came, the whole upper school looked like a beauty salon. Hair that had been worn straight all year was suddenly attacked with blow dryers, rollers, curling irons. Bitten nails magically disappeared under plastic and polish. Bits, the obvious expert in the field, was suddenly in demand as a beauty consultant. With all the attention, she came out of her shell and seemed almost her old self, rushing from one place to another, applying eyeliner with a steady hand, touching up failed hairdos, helping to stuff bras. I almost wished I could ask her help myself.

"I give up!" Marty sighed, having tried for half an hour to get my hair to bend around a borrowed curling iron. "Hair is not your strong point. It's about twice as stubborn as the rest of you!" She stood back and surveyed me critically. "You'll have to take pride in your skin tones."

I stood in front of the mirror to assess my skin tones, then the rest of my showered and powdered body, clad in bra and pants. "*Nothing* is my strong point! I'm fifteen years old and I look like a damned telephone pole!"

Marty shook those maddening black curls. "No, no, no! A *talented* damned telephone pole. Chuck doesn't love you for your body."

"No. For my convenience." I was beginning to envy Marty's decision not to go to the ball.

Marty wrapped the cord around the curling iron. "That goes both ways, you know. You like his convenience too. I'll take this back for you. I'm going to hide out in the studio for a while and see if I can get some work done."

She started out into the hall as I turned glumly back to the mirror. There was a thud, then a crash, as the curling iron hit the floor and rolled down the hall. When I got to the door Bits was standing face to face with Marty, scowling.

"Excuse me," Marty was saying. "I didn't see you there."

"Funny," Bits said, spitting the words in Marty's face like acid. "You see plenty of other things."

"Anyone sees what's too obvious to miss!"

I thought for a moment Bits was going to hit Marty, but she only stepped closer. "You'll wish you hadn't told her," she said. "One way or another, I promise you that."

Bits pulled her old terrycloth robe more tightly around her and brushed past Marty toward the lounge. Marty picked up the curling iron and came back to the room.

"That's why she's been like that all week. She thinks *I* told Priscilla."

"Told her what? Marty, what did you see?"

Marty tossed the curling iron onto my bed and shook her head. "I never said a word. It was Donald who told her." She sat on her bed, pulled her knees up to her chin, and wrapped her arms around her legs. There was a long silence. "They're working it out. They are!"

I shut the door and sat down next to her. "Tell me."

She put her head on her knees, and I thought for a moment she wasn't going to answer. Finally, she sighed. "I guess it can't hurt to tell you."

And so I learned, finally, why the Kincaids had come to Turnbull. The story was so like the story of Marty's parents, it was easy to see why Priscilla had told her. Only Priscilla wouldn't give up her art, and Donald didn't really want her to. It was just that he was a high school history teacher whose wife could make as much money selling one painting as he could earn in six months.

"She could be famous all over the world," Marty said. "And there's nothing he could ever do to match that. When he heard about the history job at Turnbull, he decided to come, even if it meant coming alone."

"What would that have solved?"

"Nothing. He was just running away from it. Then Priscilla found out she could teach here too, so she decided to come with him. She knew she could paint wherever she was, and she hoped that some time away from Chicago, where she was getting so much attention, might help. She didn't want to lose him."

"Do you think he loves her?"

"She thinks he does. But he doesn't know how to handle her success. All he's got on his side, as far as he can see it, are his looks. I guess Turnbull isn't the best place in the world to get it straightened out."

"Bits."

"Of course."

Marty was up again and pacing, her head down, closed in on herself the way she'd been in chapel that day our freshman year. "Mike, you have no idea how rough it's been here for Priscilla. To have given up so much to come here, only to have things get worse and worse. Nothing's gone the way she'd hoped it would." She stopped pacing and turned to me, her eyes full of pain. "A man whose ego is so screwed up he needs the kind of support Bits can give him—how can any woman *need* that? I can't help remembering all that trouble between Dad and my mother, all those fights. Maybe Mother really loved my dad, too, and just couldn't get it straight. And while they were fighting it out, her work was ruined. I don't know. Can it all go together? Can anybody manage both?"

She reached the window and stopped pacing, just stood, staring ahead. "They're leaving. Donald knows that if they're going to have a chance, they have to go back to Chicago and face her career head-on. So they're leaving."

For the second time since I'd known her, Marty's eyes were filled with tears. I wanted to help, but Marty isn't easy to comfort. By the time you even know she's in pain, she's gone beyond a pat on the back. Even now, she didn't cry.

"Priscilla means everything to me, Mike. Everything. What will I do when she's gone?"

She straightened up then, blinking back the tears, all her old protection back in place. The late afternoon sun touched her sweater with a soft orange glow that reflected on her face. "I'm going to the chapel for a while. When I want to cry, God helps me stop."

·ᴊ E L E V E N ᴊ·

Despite my fears, the dance was a success. "You look gorgeous," Chuck said when he saw me. And I knew that if it weren't quite the truth, it was close enough. My mother had chosen my dress, and I had to admit she'd been right about what the moss green color would do for my eyes and the Empire style would do for my waist. Even my straight hair wasn't too bad, since it was clean and soft. In the right light, there's even a golden tone in the mousy brown.

"The rest of you outdoes even your skin tones," Marty had said as I left our room to go to the gym.

I saw Bits only once, early in the evening, and what I saw was astounding. Even Chuck, who claimed to be unmoved by such shallow concerns as appearance, gaped.

"Isn't that your star cheerleader?" he asked.

"You give yourself away by remembering her," I pointed out.

But it wasn't hard to see why. She'd made her dress of white satin. It was a simple design, long and slim and cut very low in front. From the tiny straps to the soft hem, it clung to every curve of her body. Her blond hair was softly curled around her face and held away from one cheek by a large flower made of the same material as the dress. She and Dan, in the red sash of a senior squad leader, became the center of attention wherever they went.

"I only noticed her because I'm such an old-movie freak," Chuck said in defense. "She looks like Harlow!"

"Don't think she doesn't know it!" I said. For a few moments my good cheer over my own appearance faded. Everything faded next to Bits.

"It's not just her," Chuck observed. "All the girls look good tonight."

He was right. Even Willie, her bowlegs hidden under an old-fashioned-looking dress of gingham and lace, looked feminine and almost pretty.

"If you only knew how hard we work."

Chuck grinned. "Note the dress uniforms! Don't think you have a monopoly on vanity." He snapped his fingers. "I'll bet that's why we've spent so much of history at war! Men needed uniforms to impress women. *Voila!* Armies! And once you have an army, you might as well have a war."

We danced for a while, then went outside for a walk. During the Spring Ball couples are allowed to walk on the campus if the weather's warm enough. There are lanterns hung in the trees—"to make things look romantic," I explained.

"To keep Emily Turnbull's girls in the light," Chuck countered.

"There are always bushes," I said, "for an enterprising cadet."

"You're forgetting the saltpeter!"

"Myth!"

As we walked beside the breakwater, listening to the water slap against the rocks, Chuck took my hand. "I envy you this campus," he said. "I envy you the lake. There's something about so much water—even at night, when it's just a vast darkness."

"Everybody comes out here when they're depressed."

"It's because we came from the sea. It's like crawling on your mother's lap when you're little. The sound of water is our mother's heartbeat." He laughed as if his seriousness had embarrassed him.

Ignoring the newness of my dress, I climbed onto a rock and pulled him after me. "I'll show you where *I* come to listen to the heartbeat."

We stayed on the breakwater for a long time, not talking much, just watching the lake as the moon rose over it.

Finally he looked at his watch and groaned. "It's time to go back. We should dance the last dance at least."

So we went back, laughing about the marks the damp rock had left on my dress.

"They used to look for grass stains on a girl's dress," Chuck said as we tried to look casual while we kept my back to the wall of the gym. "I wonder what Emily Turnbull would have to say about rock stains."

This time, when we went to Chuck's bus, he kissed me until someone tapped him firmly on the shoulder. It was Miss Clawson, her eyes full of a grandmotherly twinkle despite her frown.

"Let's not delay Southport's departure," she said, and turned me toward the building.

"Gorgeous!" Chuck called, as he jumped onto the bus. "Gorgeous!" I heard again as I started back.

As I climbed the stairs toward the dormitory, I felt somehow light. I hardly noticed the girls who bustled around me, chattering and laughing. I hardly noticed anything until I bumped into Priscilla Kincaid standing at the doorway of the dorm.

"Have you seen Elizabeth?" she asked, and I had to think for a moment to realize who she meant.

"Bits? No, not since early this evening. Why?"

"No one knows where she is. I've just checked her room and she isn't there." She saw the question in my face. "We don't know where Dan is either. They're holding his bus—the other bus has already gone."

Since I had no information, she went back downstairs, pushing through the noisy groups of girls coming up.

Marty, in her robe and pajamas, met me in the hall. "Did you see Priscilla?"

I nodded. "You think Bits ran away?"

"Never. Turnbull's too important to her."

She was right. Bits might not like being a scholarship student, but at least she was at Turnbull, and that's where she wanted to be.

By the time everyone was back in the dorm, Bits' disappearance was the sole topic of conversation. Clusters of girls, still in their long dresses, stood in the hallway, whispering. Everyone wanted to be there when she showed up, "if she ever does," someone said.

Someone else was sure she'd run away. "I'll bet they eloped or something."

"Nobody elopes anymore. They just run away and live together. Do you suppose they'd let Dan graduate if he was living with Bits?"

"Why doesn't everybody just go to bed!" wailed Jeannie. She was doing her best not to cry, but her face was pink with the effort. No one moved.

It was probably half an hour before the door opened and Mrs. Kincaid ushered Bits through it. Bits' hair was disheveled, her white flower was gone, and her dress was streaked with mud.

"Go to your rooms!" Mrs. Kincaid said, in a voice none of us had heard before. We went.

At breakfast the next morning everyone was talking about Bits and Dan. The bus had been held up for half an hour—the first time such a thing had ever happened. Bits was refusing to answer questions about where they had been, and was sitting at her table, head high, ignoring the talk that buzzed around the dining room. I found myself wondering how she really felt. Everyone knew she was to see Stoney at two o'clock, and bets were being taken that she'd be expelled. Knowing how she felt about being at Turnbull, I couldn't imagine why she'd taken such a risk.

"It's disgusting!" I heard Jeannie say. "You're like vultures."

"Almost enough to make you lose your appetite," someone said.

Even at the Penwomen meeting the subject of Bits and Dan came up so often that Miss Engles dismissed us in disgust. I took my time gathering up my things in case she'd ask me to stay, but she barely noticed me, so I left with the others. It was still early, and the air was warm; almost without noticing where I was going, I found myself back on the breakwater where Chuck and I had come during the dance. I kept thinking about sitting there with Chuck, not talking, just being happy to be there together, my hand in his, watching the moon's path on the water. I could have sat there like that forever.

But somehow I couldn't put that together with love. What I felt with Chuck was easy and comfortable and warm. The nearest thing I could think of was the way Marty and I would sometimes know what the other was feeling without having to put it into words. The way I felt about Chuck just didn't seem to fit the way Bits had been acting about Donald Kincaid. Or the chance she took for some extra time with Dan. There weren't any bells ringing or fireworks. There had been something new, though. There had been the kiss, and that light feeling I'd had on the stairs. I could get that feeling back just remembering it, and even though it didn't seem wonderful enough to be love, I stayed there for a while watching the color patterns changing on the lake, thinking about Chuck.

Finally, the afternoon chill drove me off the breakwater. I hadn't worn a jacket to the Penwomen meeting. On the way back to the buildings, I had to pass a small formal garden, surrounded by boxwood hedges, whose stone fountain was crumbling, its pool choked with debris. It's been neglected for years, and hardly anyone ever goes there, except occasionally to find some privacy behind its green walls. As I got close to it I heard voices, so I started to make a detour around it when I recognized Bits' voice, loud and grating and filled with fury. I stopped in spite of myself.

". . . so if you think you've won, you're crazy! I will *not* leave Turnbull. I'd do anything to stay!"

"We don't want you to leave." The other voice, calm and rational and so quiet I had to strain to hear, was Priscilla Kincaid's.

"You're so damned sure of yourself! You use that 'we' like a weapon. Well, just wait and see how it holds up. I know what Stoney planned to do this afternoon. But I stopped her."

Priscilla's voice rose. "*You* did?"

"I did. I told her something that shocked even Stoney." Bits' voice was triumphant.

"I don't know what you told Miss Stonehill, Elizabeth, but it was *I* who kept you from being expelled."

Bits laughed. "Oh, sure. You're so anxious for me to stay!"

Priscilla's voice sounded tired. "I don't care one way or another, actually."

"You want me away from your precious Donald and you know it!"

"I have nothing to fear from you, Elizabeth. I told Miss Stonehill that I didn't think last night was serious enough to warrant expelling you, and she finally agreed."

There was a slight pause. When Bits spoke again, her voice was slightly less loud, slightly less sure. "I don't believe you. You didn't keep Stoney from expelling me, *I* did." There was another pause and I heard a bird singing somewhere over my head. "After all, why should a poor scholarship girl suffer over being a few minutes late for a bus when a rich kid is allowed to break up a marriage?"

I heard the words, but for a moment I didn't know what they meant. Suddenly, the meaning was all too clear. Overhead, the bird was still singing.

"What do you mean by that?" Priscilla's voice was sharp.

"You think people don't know about you and the Princess? You think people haven't noticed all those Saturday afternoons in the studio? The fact that she calls you by your first name? The strain between you and Donald?"

I felt sick. For a moment, it seemed too still, nearly dark, like the sky before a tornado. I blinked and was almost surprised to see the sun still slanting across the grass at my feet. I barely made out what Priscilla said then, almost in a whisper:

"You did not say such a thing to Miss Stonehill."

The triumph was back in Bits' voice. "Didn't I? And let's

see you deny it. You spent a weekend together in Detroit. We'll see who's leaving Turnbull. We'll see."

Bits came out of the garden, then, her head high, her shoulders back. There was no sound from the other side of the hedge. I dared not move, for fear I'd be heard, so I stood there, my head spinning, my hands damp. Marty's "dark and light" echoed over and over.

I felt as if I'd been frozen there for hours when Priscilla emerged from the garden, looking thinner and more fragile than ever, a sketchbook under her arm, her shoulders hunched forward. I thought how different the two were—Bits with her fresh good looks, all that smug self-confidence; Priscilla, so different, so vulnerable-looking.

When she was gone, I started to move, then stopped. The full impact of what Bits had said hit me. If she repeated it all over school, everything would seem to fit. Not just the Saturdays in the studio, the weekend in Detroit, but everything. Marty refusing to go to the Spring Ball. Her lack of interest in Turnbull's social life. Marty would have no defense against Bits' story because nobody really knew her. As different as Priscilla Kincaid was from the rest of the faculty, Marty was from the other girls. And differences have to be explained. How convenient an explanation this would be.

A robin fluttered to the grass in front of me and began hopping along, its head cocked, its eyes bright. I stamped my foot and watched it fly away. "No worm for you this time," I thought, and then I began to run.

When Miss Engles came to her door, I didn't wait to be invited in, just pushed past her and collapsed into the leather chair, gasping for breath. This time when I started to cry there wasn't any confusion. This time I was crying for Marty, and it seemed as if I would never stop.

❧ TWELVE ❧

I did stop, of course, huddled in the chair with the Kleenexes Miss Engles had given me, holding them against my eyes, not just to soak up the tears, but to keep out—what? Whatever would be waiting when I went back to the dorm?

Miss Engles listened then, shaking her head, her face grave but not as concerned as I thought she should be. "It wouldn't be the first time we've had a story like that to deal with," she said. "It's a little ironic that this one began with the Kincaids. It was to help avoid just this kind of problem that they were brought here in the first place."

"What will Marty do?"

"Probably what she did when she was first called the Princess. She'll probably ignore it."

"I guess so. But what about Stoney?"

"I doubt that she'll take the word of a student in trouble over that of a faculty member. Besides, she knows what else is happening there."

"So we're supposed to pretend nothing's wrong!"

"Why don't you wait and see what you're really dealing with? The world *has* changed a little. It might not be so terrible."

By the time I got back to the dorm, I'd at least begun to be-

lieve that this could be handled the way Marty had handled everything else. She was strong enough to ignore gossip, especially since it wasn't true. I didn't for a minute doubt that Bits had
been spreading the story; she'd want as much support as she
could get. I hoped Marty would be in the room. Better to hear it
from me than from someone else.

I saw it halfway down the hall, Scotch-taped to our door. But
it wasn't until I was closer that I could tell what it was—a poster for "gay lib." Marty was sitting on her bed, her face grim.
And it was obvious that I was too late.

"I'm sorry," she said, as I ripped the poster off the door.
"Priscilla was here a while ago. Bits is telling everyone that she
and I . . . I'm sorry."

"Sorry? Why?" And then I understood. How stupid I'd
been, so worried about Marty that I hadn't for a moment considered what it might say about me. What could be true about
Marty, why not about Marty's roommate, best friend, whatever
else? If Marty and Priscilla, why not Marty and me? And if
Marty and me? Incredible. I'd gone straight to Miss Engles. I
could only hope no one had seen me.

"It isn't your fault," I said, and wished I had Marty's
strength. "What'll we do?"

"What *can* we do? We just go on the way we always have.
What people want to believe they will believe, and nothing we
can do or say is going to make any difference."

"Terrific."

"Yeah."

It had begun already, but just then, as we sat on our beds
and wondered what would happen, we had no way of knowing
what the next weeks would be like. By dinner time the story
had reached everyone. Nobody was saying anything yet, but we
could tell by the way they looked, by the way they moved away

from us in the hall. And by the next day, the comments had begun, and the notes.

I picked up my biology book in the study hall and saw a bit of paper sticking out between the pages. "Go home," I read, "before you give us all a bad name." In the corner of the blackboard in the Latin room was chalked a heart with our initials. Miss Hershberger erased it without a word. But all through Latin I had the feeling she was looking at us differently. Already I was having trouble deciding how much I was seeing and how much was only my imagination. At lunch Jeannie and Bits had moved from the table; but Scovie, Willie, and Tag were still there. "At least I can count on them," I thought, as the conversation stayed carefully neutral. "They'll give us a buffer." Twice I noticed Tag looking at me, but when I caught her eye, she became suddenly interested in her bowl of soup. She's embarrassed by it, that's all, I assured myself. But I couldn't finish my lunch.

It was Monday, my day to meet with Miss Engles. I didn't go. At least at a Penwomen meeting there were all those others there. It was almost like having leprosy—anyone we went near might be in danger too. Marty, refusing to change anything, went to the studio after school to work on her designs. Feeling sick, I headed for Scovie's room. What I needed was a dose of her humor. Or Willie's pragmatism. Anything that wasn't that look of suspicion, almost fear, I was seeing everywhere.

When I got to their room, the door was half open, and their voices reached me in the hall. I never thought to stop, to listen, never thought to give them a chance to be ready for me. I just pushed open the door.

The silence was instantaneous. Three sets of eyes were on me, and three faces were set in that kind of shock I could only associate with a kid at a cookie jar. It was too late not to be there. Too late not to see what I had seen.

Scovie was the first to recover. "Mike!" she said, sounding like a salesman. "We were just—"

"I know," I said. "Just talking about me—"

"You'll have to admit, it explains a lot."

For some reason I became aware of the gold earrings Tag always wore—small, plain rings that fit close to her earlobes. I'd seen them so often, I usually didn't even notice them.

I looked at Scovie and she looked away. Willie was busy smoothing a wrinkle from her bedspread. "Does it?" I asked and turned back into the hall.

"How could it be?" I asked myself as I went down the hall to our room. How could the D.E.T.s be over, just like that? With one lie, one person trying to save herself from something she didn't even need to be afraid of. And my so-called family was gone.

"Second time," I thought. "One car accident, one lie." And what was left? If only Scovie would refuse to believe it, I'd be okay. Just Scovie. Just the person I'd lived with for two years. She *had* to know the truth. And what had happened to that way Tag had always had of seeing the truth. What was she seeing now?

"I guess I don't know what friendship is," I said to Marty later, when I'd told her. "What about loyalty? What about believing in people?"

"I don't know," she said. "Maybe they just need some time."

"And what about us?"

"What *about* us? We know the truth. And Stoney knows it too."

"I don't hear her making an assembly announcement about it."

"I doubt that she wants to get into it. Maybe she just figures it'll go away."

But it didn't. The days dragged by, and even Scovie kept avoiding me, looking the other way whenever I tried to catch her eye. There seemed to be a conspiracy of silence from anyone who could have stopped it, could have told the truth. Bits was campused, and soon the story was that Stoney had been bought by Sheffield money, letting Marty and Priscilla go on working together so that Marty would stay, keeping everything quiet to avoid a scandal.

Miss Engles stopped me after class the next week and told me to come to her room after school. I refused, and she took my arm in a grip so strong it hurt. "If every student who spent an hour with a teacher were suspect, who'd be safe? Be here after school!"

That afternoon I sat on the windowsill on the far side of the room and looked out across the lawns and the flower gardens while she said all the sensible things I wanted to believe but couldn't anymore. "This too shall pass?" I asked.

"Yes."

"And will I look back and laugh at it someday?"

She sat on a chair next to me. "You may not laugh, Mike. But you'll get through it. Exams are coming up. Nobody's going to have time to keep up the kind of harassment you've had to put up with. And after that is summer. Even if it were true, they'd be bound to lose interest."

"Somehow that's hardly a comfort!"

"Isn't there anyone who hasn't changed toward you?"

I looked out at the neatly manicured gardens and thought

about it. My impulse was to say no. But there were people who hadn't changed. Most of the members of Penwomen, even some of the sophomores. I'd been so preoccupied with the D.E.T.s, and with whoever had been leaving the notes and the posters, I hadn't noticed. "A few," I admitted. "But what good does that do when my best friends have turned on me?"

"Think about it. They're the ones who have something to lose themselves. This kind of gossip spreads, as you've discovered. From Marty to you, why not from you to them? Give them more time."

In the silence of the room I could hear the clock over her desk do its little jump from one minute to the next. I'd never thought about anyone being scared. Miss Engles stood up, and I discovered that I really did feel a little better.

"How's Marty taking it?" she asked.

"I'm not sure. She isn't exactly the emotional type. Everything stays pretty hidden."

She shook her head. "It would be better if she'd let herself feel it."

"She spends a lot of time in chapel," I said, and wished that I knew how to get comfort that way. "She says God helps her stop crying."

"You can't stop crying until you start," Miss Engles said.

Later, I thought about Marty not feeling it, and I knew that was wrong. She had such a habit of control that what she felt didn't show much. But she felt it, all right.

Sometimes, since it had started, I'd catch something in her eyes I'd never seen before. It was like a shadow, a darkening of the light I was used to. She would seem to be absorbing something she was studying, or doing her class assignments as easily as ever, but I could tell her concentration wasn't what it had been. When she'd get out her sketchbook, there wasn't the old sparkle in her eyes. For the first time since I'd known her, she began to treat art almost like work.

The week before exams she got a note from the gallery in Detroit that had taken some of her charcoals, telling her that two had been sold. It was her first professional sale, at a gallery where her work was competing with the work of adults. But it didn't really seem to penetrate.

By the time exams began, Miss Engles' prediction had come true. The talk had finally ended. Even Bits was so busy trying to catch up that she didn't have time to fan the fires.

And then, the night before our last exam, Scovie knocked at our door. When she came in she stood for a minute, shifting her weight from foot to foot, looking almost as if her body had brought her there against her will. Finally, she managed a sheepish grin. "I guess we ought to know Bits better than to believe everything she says."

Marty didn't look up from her book. "I guess."

Scovie turned to me. "I'm sorry, Mike. I guess I lived with you long enough to know better."

I thought about how I'd felt, standing in her room, knowing for the first time what Bits' lie had done. I couldn't be very sympathetic about Scovie's discomfort now. But I'd lived with her a long time too, and I didn't want to believe that didn't count for something. "It's okay," I said. And I knew that even if it weren't really okay, at least it was beginning to be better.

For Marty, though, nothing seemed to get better. I suspected that it hadn't been the talk that had hurt her so much as knowing that Priscilla was leaving. No matter how wrong Bits had been about them, I kept remembering what Marty had said—

"She's everything to me. Everything." With Priscilla, Marty's life had been turned around, the dream she had had to keep hidden had not only come into the open, it had already begun to come true. Maybe Bits had believed her story. It would seem to explain what hardly anybody could understand. For Bits, only sex could make such a powerful connection between people. But I knew better, and I watched as the end of the year came closer and the shadow in Marty's eyes began to put out the light entirely.

Stoney announced that our old art teacher, Miss Hamilton, was coming back to Turnbull. The relative she had quit to take care of had died. Everything seemed to be going backward.

The morning we were to leave, it was raining, a steady June rain. Marty got up for early Mass and didn't come to breakfast. When I got to the room to finish packing, she wasn't there, her packing was barely begun. I checked the studio—it was the only place she'd moved out of. Her easel was empty, her sketches were gone from the walls, her smock wasn't on its hook by the door. I looked in the chapel and found only shadows and the smell of the lilies of the valley on the altar for graduation. On my way back to the dorm I stopped at the window at the top of the stairs to look out at the lake and saw Marty and Priscilla walking together, ignoring the rain. Clearly, Marty didn't need me.

My mother came before Marty got back, complaining about having to load the car in the rain. Almost immediately, she started in on me about the "junk" I'd accumulated during the year. It was our eternal going-home scene, except that this time I had too much else on my mind to pay much attention to it. I sent her off, still clutching her umbrella, to see Miss Engles, who had promised to put in a few good words about my writing.

Marty finally came in, soaked to the skin. I handed her a towel to dry her hair and sat on my trunk, watching her. Her face seemed a little more relaxed, her eyes a little less cloudy. "You won't believe what Priscilla told me," she said. "Bits has to leave Turnbull after all."

"But Stoney said——"

"Stoney didn't do it. Bits did it herself. She flunked two subjects and lost her scholarship."

I started to laugh at the irony of it all, but then I remembered the first two years, the secret pockets, the keys to the kitchen, and all the D.E.T.s private parties—and I didn't laugh. Where would Bits be next year? How would she explain? "Maybe she'll be better off somewhere where she won't feel so poor," I said.

Marty stopped rubbing her hair. "Bits will always find someone to envy." She peeled off her wet shirt and jeans. "Priscilla really thinks she and Donald may have a chance now. And in some ways it's thanks to Bits. Donald was so appalled at what Bits did that she thinks it might have shaken him out of himself a little. Maybe he's beginning to see that there's something between them worth saving. Anyway, he's going back to Chicago with her and he says he's willing to try."

Marty pulled a T-shirt over her head and dug a dry pair of jeans out of the open suitcase on her bed. When she spoke again, I could see the beginnings of the old sparkle. "She's found me a teacher for next year, right here in Graylander. His name is John Justin—Priscilla seems to respect his work. And think of it, Mike. A man! What do you suppose they'll say to that?"

"I hear bisexuality is very popular these days!"

And we were laughing—the first real laugh in weeks.

My mother came in then, and we got involved in congratulations over the St. Mark's windows. Then everything became boxes and dripping umbrellas. Before we knew it, we were standing by the car, umbrellas bumping, unable to think of anything to say as Mom got into the car.

"To next year," Marty said.

We managed an awkward hug, almost without worrying if anyone was watching, and I got into the car, where Mom was revving the engine impatiently.

As we drove through Turnbull's gates, I looked back at Marty, standing in the driveway under her umbrella, waving until we turned out of sight.

"Miss Engles tells me you've had quite a year," Mom said, and I looked sideways at the familiar profile, thinking how much there was about that year she'd never know.

"Yeah," I muttered, and thought about Marty standing in the driveway in the rain.

❧ THIRTEEN ❧

During the summer I worked in the library in Waterford part-time, enough to give me something to do, a reason to be out of the house and plenty of time to read. Otherwise, it was pretty much a summer of letters.

Chère MICHELLE,

It was not *wise* of me to take a job with a lawn service. I'm sunburned almost to death! You'd love the way my freckles give texture to the beety shade of my face. Besides that, I've got blisters on my hands and my heels and I'm developing an allergy to grass. HELP!

If you don't have plans for the Fourth, maybe we could spend it together. My father was so turned on about my grades (have I sold out?) that he actually gave me a car. It's not much, but it'll hang together long enough to get me to Waterford. I await your reply with bated breath (except when the grass makes me sneeze!).

Votre ami,
CHUCK

My mother was even more pleased about Chuck than she

had been about Marty. She gave up her usual summer cam-
paign to arrange something between me and one of the Waterford guys I hardly knew. Chuck came down a few times, and
we had the kind of friendly, easy time we'd had at the Spring
Ball. We parked some, but mostly we talked—about Turnbull
and Southport, about war and peace, about religion, about writ-
ers, everything.

Marty wrote, too. In fact, we wrote every other day, our letters getting crossed in the mail and half of what we wanted to
say seeming to get lost between all the changes of subject and
mistimed questions and answers. Still, the letters kept us in
touch.

DEAR MIKE,

Priscilla has come and gone and even Jane didn't know
how to handle it. I think she and Dad were both a little
frightened of her, can you imagine? Of course she was wearing a practically see-through billowy peasant dress and those
shoes with the ribbons that cross all the way up to her knees,
plus the usual feathers. My poor father didn't know what to
make of her, especially when he found out she could actually
converse like an intelligent being. Charlie loved her on sight!
That's probably what finally won Dad over. Jane just melted
into the background and waited for her to go away.

We took the designs to the St. Mark's board (great success!), then got Charlie and lunch and had a picnic at the
park. What a silly afternoon. Like that day last spring. We
swung on swings and waded in a stream and all three of us
acted about Charlie's age. She invited me to come to Chicago
in August, and Dad actually said yes. Jane did her best to
stop it. Wasn't that the week we'd planned to visit her par-

ents? But of course there were no such plans. Priscilla promised to introduce me to some gallery people there, too. I'm working on a series of charcoals to take when I go. I started them there at the park, and one of them is of her and Charlie in the stream. It's my best ever!

How's the library work going? And how can I tell you what I think of Sylvia Plath when I haven't read her poetry? Priscilla has, and she says fifteen-year-old female artists should stay away from people like her. And Anne Sexton! If you're going to read all those doom people, what kind of a year will it be? You'll be throwing yourself out of windows. Find somebody happy! What ever happened to Millay?

August! Chicago! Then back. Maybe even without Priscilla I'll survive. She says this Justin will be good for me, whatever that means!

Love,

The Masked Gladiator

By the time I got that letter, I'd already stopped reading Sylvia Plath and Anne Sexton. I felt somehow put off by their poetry, as if they were dealing with things I didn't even want to know about. I kept writing in my journal and wondered what Miss Engles would say if she could see me in a corner of the library reading spy novels. I'd degenerated right into escape reading, and it was fun.

And then it was time to go back to school. I was almost frightened the morning we left home and started for Graylander. What would it be like to be back? How would Scovie and the others act after the summer? How much would everyone remember? As we turned in at the gate, my hands were sweating, and I hoped Marty would be there. I wanted to see her before I had to deal with anyone else.

As it turned out, Scovie was the first person I saw. Being juniors, we were at last granted the privilege, shared with the seniors, of living on the first floor of the dormitory building. No more flights of stairs to struggle up with all that luggage. But there was still the door from the stairway hall. When I came in, Scovie was trying to get it open without dropping either of the huge battered suitcases she was holding or her hockey stick. I went around her and held it open. When she was through, she put down her suitcases and her hockey stick after all, to hug me. It wasn't the old, screaming, back-thumping hug, but it was real, and I relaxed. The D.E.T.s were finished, but I knew at least we'd be able to face each other.

Marty came later, and instead of unpacking, we sat on the bare mattresses in our new room and talked. It seemed strange that after all those letters we could still have so much to say, but there was a difference, being able to talk face to face and see past the words. We were still talking when Scovie came in, stomping and grumbling. When she and Willie and Tag had had to give up the three-person room, she had volunteered to take the smallest room in the senior dorm as a single.

"I've been sabotaged!" she said. "They've given me a roommate! A lousy new girl!"

When we had left for the summer, the only new girl expected in the junior class was to room with Jeannie, who was so distraught over losing Bits that she couldn't face the thought of living with anyone she knew. During the summer another junior had been accepted, and they'd turned the small room into a double.

"They know perfectly well that room's too small for two people." Scovie groaned. "I practically have to move my bed to get the closet door open. And of course *she* took the good bed with the firm mattress I'd picked out. I'll have to get a lousy bed-board! You should see the furniture they moved in there. Relics from Emily's time, every bit of it! At least she hadn't unpacked yet, so I got my choice of dressers and desks. I'm going to *hate* her!"

Marty was unmoved by Scovie's tragedy. "Why do you think that?"

"Her trunk—the one on *my* mattress—is covered with stickers from a camp called Mendota. With that many stickers you've got to figure she likes it there."

"What's the matter with that? You can't be prejudiced against jocks. You *are* one!" I reminded her.

But she was in no mood to be reasoned with. She'd have hated Willie if they'd moved her in without warning. "Well, I'm not a camper! And then there's her name. Sylva Hart. What kind of a name is that?"

"Sylvia?" I asked, thinking I'd heard wrong.

"No. Syl-va. There's no *i*—I checked it twice."

Marty got up to begin unpacking. "Maybe we should wait and see who we feel sorriest for. You or her."

Scovie frowned. "I'm going to see Mrs. Martin. Maybe this Sylva can be moved someplace else."

When she had stormed off down the hall to look for our dorm mother, sounding like Willie in her cowboy boots, Marty shook her head. "You sure can't envy anyone who's going to get a reception like that. I wonder why she was accepted so late?"

That evening we all met Sylva Hart, and I decided that her name was the only unusual thing about her. She was very ordinary-looking, it seemed to me, stocky, about my height, with dark brown hair cut short and brushed back. The depth of her tan showed that she'd spent plenty of time outdoors. She soon informed everyone that Camp Mendota was a very exclusive sailing camp where she'd spent ten weeks every summer since her tenth birthday. It was clear she considered herself a top-notch sailor. She'd never been to boarding school before; she'd gone to a very classy suburban high school near Detroit where she'd been a straight-*A* student until her parents got embroiled in an especially nasty divorce suit and she'd been sent to Turnbull to get her out of their way. The only thing that impressed me about Sylva Hart at the time was the way she'd managed to tell everyone so many good things about herself in such a short time. She had even managed to make her parents' divorce and their desire to get rid of her seem to be an honor. Quite a performance. I was glad not to be in Scovie's place.

At the first Penwomen meeting I was chosen to be editor of the literary magazine we had decided to publish. Immediately I began to picture myself as a new Harriet Monroe, finding brilliant new literary talent and introducing it to the world. I imagined a salon full of artistic types all currying favor with me to get into my magazine.

In the meantime, I got Marty named art editor, then wondered if they'd made me editor just so Marty would do the artwork. Obviously, my self-confidence index was not improving, and I couldn't really believe in my Harriet Monroe image. But the skies were clear, the weather beautiful, and after the troubles of the spring, this seemed to be the beginning of the best year yet. If Scovie, Willie, and Tag were not "family" anymore, there was Marty, and Penwomen, and Miss Engles. I was finished with Latin—forever—and French was a snap in comparison. Even chemistry and math weren't bad. Life stretched out ahead like a series of steps from darkness to light, getting better and better.

Mr. Justin, Marty's new teacher, turned out to be as good for her as Priscilla had said he'd be. Instead of taking her on from where she was, he made her go back and work on basic techniques again. And instead of driving her mad with boredom, his assignments showed her weaknesses Priscilla had ignored. She actually enjoyed the work, and I was reminded of the way Miss Engles taught writing: "You can't add gargoyles till you've built the plain, solid walls." I particularly liked his methods because instead of keeping Marty at an easel in the studio, he sent her outside with her sketchbook. So we went together, Marty with her sketchbook, I with my journal. On the breakwater, at the beach, almost always by the lake.

And though I noticed that Marty would withdraw inside herself from time to time, the clouds coming down again as if she were remembering the troubles of the spring, we were together again, and it seemed to be all that mattered. Everything seemed easy and right.

✾ FOURTEEN ✾

Picnic Day! I opened my eyes to sunlight filtering through the orange and yellow leaves of the maple tree outside the window—the light alive like the reflection of sun on water. Indian summer. Corn stalks and pumpkins and a tang of apples. Geese gabbling by in the long, wavering V overhead. The fishy, weedy smell of the lake and the scent of dried leaves as they crunch under the bike tires. Marty and I and Miss Engles, bringing up the tag end of the riders—seniors way off ahead somewhere, Scovie and Willie and Sylva even farther, beating them—and the three of us coming along slowly, breathing in and looking. Then that catch of breath as we came into a tunnel of light under yellow hickory trees. A miracle of a day! I kept riding off the road—how could I look anywhere except at the trees, the sky, their colors vibrating inside my head like plucked guitar strings. A late picnic this year that we're allowed to ride the ten miles. An omen. Our picnic on the best day of the fall!

Here we are in the middle of it all, trying to catch it before it goes. Now. Here. Sitting in the leaves. Mr. Justin came with the buses so Marty wouldn't miss her Saturday morning, sent her with chalks to catch the color and the light, himself walking on the beach with Miss Engles.

Sounds. Someone has discovered the vines. Tarzans plunging down the hillside when the vines come loose. Squirrels chattering to send us off out of their world. Seagulls. Ducks somewhere behind me. Marty's chalk—little squiffs of sound against the paper.

How to catch this tree in words? We walked the park, passing up the scarlet of the sumac, the hickory gold, the dogwood. There was a moment when the path curved and there was a slope of green, curving beside the trickle of stream and two enormous trees, almost all gold, patches of brown and green around them and a breeze that scattered the bits of gold—a drift of golden snow across the line of green. Pieces of the sun falling. We stopped, and I wanted to break out of time, to save the moment, when I felt alive— like Millay: "My soul is almost out of me."

Walking on, underneath those trees, kicking at acorns, crushing the dry oak leaves, and then *finding this tree*. This maple, bigger than a mountain, on fire, each leaf like a flame, from red to yellow—each leaf! Marty cursing now. No chalks can catch the color. "Oils! Acrylics! Even blood!" And then we're laughing. Imagine her painting with her blood, me writing with mine. What is there about October?

We have to go. For lunch. Lunch, when we would rather stop time. Impossible!

❦ ❦

After lunch we had to stay for the class games, the sack race, egg toss, wheelbarrow race. Scovie, Willie, and Sylva had disgraced the seniors by getting to the park first, beating even

Miss Holcomb, who thought she was at the head of the line, and then we skunked them in the games. It was the juniors' day. After that we were free again until four, when the riders had to start back. We went off toward the beach, and Marty pointed to where Miss Engles and Mr. Justin were standing at the water line, their heads bent together, deep in conversation. Mr. Justin, in corduroys and flannel shirt, his graying hair catching the sun, bent to pick up a stone, then skipped it expertly over the slight waves.

"Ah-ha!" Marty said.

"Beware of jumping to conclusions!" I warned.

Marty nodded wisely. "But think of the paintings in her apartment. She knows art! And today is Picnic Day! Anything can happen on Picnic Day!"

We left them alone and followed a new trail through the woods. Marty wanted to catch the change from morning to afternoon light, so we were trying to find another spectacular tree when we came, suddenly, to the boundary of the park. There was a barn behind a double strand of barbed wire.

"Come on, Mike! I'll sketch the barn."

We climbed between the wires and went around the side of a ramshackle barn that leaned at a crazy angle toward the fence. Marty sat on an empty crate and I paced around, expecting someone to come up behind us any minute. I kept slipping into the shelter of the trees and bushes near the fence, trying to decide where the house that must go with the barn might be so I could keep a watch. Finally, I spotted a line of wash strung across an overgrown, junk-strewn yard. Behind it was the house, its sagging, peeling back porch nearly hidden by a half-dead hedge. I stationed myself between the house and Marty's back as she bent over the sketch pad on her lap. I doubted the farmer would understand that we had only come to draw his barn.

When I'd stood there as long as I could, I went back and found Marty putting away her chalks. "Finished. Those muted colors are much better with chalks than that tree." She stood up and then grabbed my arm. "Mike, look!"

On the other side of a huge, straggly honeysuckle bush I saw a row of trees, bent over with the weight of their hundreds of apples. "Let's go. There's nothing like an apple fresh off the tree!"

We crept along the fence line, keeping out of sight as well as possible, until we were among the apple trees. It was a small orchard, smelling of autumn, of ripe apples and windfalls. I jumped for an apple, expecting to hear the whine of a bullet past my ear. But there was no sound except the steady knocking of a woodpecker behind us in the park. I had taken my first bite, letting the juice run down my chin, when Marty swung herself up into the nearest tree.

"Take off your sweatshirt!" she called. "We'll need something to carry them in."

I pulled off my sweatshirt and spread it on the ground beneath the tree. She dropped apples to me while I glanced over my shoulder every few seconds.

The voice came just after Marty dropped to the ground, while I was tying the sleeves of my sweatshirt to make a kind of sack. "Get out of there, you thieving kids! I've got a shotgun!"

I dropped the sweatshirt and ran, imagining the sting of buckshot in my rear, clutching my half-eaten apple in one hand like some kind of charm.

When Marty caught up with me, the sweatshirt full of apples

in her arms, she was laughing. "What's the matter with you, dropping the apples? You want to get shot for nothing?" She put them down by the fence. "I have to go back for my sketch-book."

I took her arm. "Are you nuts? Leave it. He really might shoot!"

She laughed again and pulled away. "He's bluffing. You don't shoot a person over a few apples. Be right back."

I crawled between the barbed wires and sat against a tree, waiting to hear the gun, Marty's scream, a siren, something. But the only thing I heard was Marty coming back, doing her best to run bent double, clutching her sketchbook and chalk. Her face was white.

"Get me through," she shouted. "He *does* have a gun!"

She tore her sweatshirt on the barbed wire, but we didn't stop to check the damage. We just ran, dropping apples out of my shirt as we went, until we'd reached the beach. Then we stopped to get our breath and count our loot.

"More than a dozen still," Marty said when she'd counted them. "No telling how many we lost. I guess I got a little carried away."

"No wonder he has a shotgun, with an orchard next to a state park. He probably loses half his crop this way every year."

"I refuse to give in to guilt. These are too good!"

We sat on a fallen log at the edge of the woods, crunched the tart, juicy apples, and watched the lake do its own color miracle—stripes of green and blue, dotted with white caps as far as we could see.

When it was time to get back to the bikes, we divided the apples and wrapped them in both our sweatshirts. Miss Engles gave us one of her penetrating looks when we dumped them into the bike baskets to put our sweatshirts back on, but she didn't say anything.

The ride home was slower for everyone, so we stayed pretty well together, in a long, wavering line like the geese. It had been a good day, and no one was in any rush to get back. As we pedaled along, I watched the leaves change in the deeper color of the setting sun.

When I nearly ran off the road again, looking at another maple tree, Miss Engles dropped back to ride with us. "Now I know what I'm along for," she said.

I took an apple from my basket and handed it to her.

"God sure knows something about tastes," Marty said as she crunched into another apple. "Strawberries are right for spring and peaches for summer, but there's no flavor in the world that fits this time of year like an apple."

I threw a core into the cornfield we were passing. "So Adam and Eve lost us the garden in October?"

"I never thought of that," she said. "I guess so." We rode on for a while, Miss Engles and Marty finishing their apples, and then Marty spoke again. "It fits, you know. Gardens are finished then. It was an end—but it was a beginning too, in some ways. Just like fall. October and apples. I like that!"

We rode so slowly on the way back that it was almost dark when we reached the bike racks in the parking lot. Miss Engles had turned off as we passed Faculty House.

Sylva, who had been riding with Scovie and Willie again, came over as Marty was taking her apples out of the basket. "I've got something to ask you about," she said, and pulled Marty off toward the dorm.

I stood for a moment, taking a last breath of the day, and

turned to see Jeannie looking after Sylva and Marty. I tossed her my last apple.

"That Sylva Hart's a strange person," she said.

"Why do you say that?"

"Just something she said at the picnic today. While you guys were off 'acquiring' these, she asked who I thought were the best friends in the class." Jeannie glanced at me sideways and took a bite of the apple. "I told her you and Marty."

I thought for a moment of last spring and then shook it away.

"And then she said, 'I'll have that broken up in less than a month.'"

I looked to see if Jeannie was kidding. She wasn't. "What do you think she meant by that?" I asked.

"Who knows? I told you it was strange."

"Yeah. Strange." The wind off the lake seemed to bite through my sweatshirt as Jeannie and I walked through the darkness toward the dorm.

~❧ FIFTEEN ❧~

I soon found that an editor doesn't have a lot of time for writing poetry. Time seemed to move at a new pace; the ticking of the clock by my bed became almost an obsession. Study hall would be filled with French and math and chemistry, then reading all the writing that came in for the magazine. It began to seem as if I were doing nothing but reading what other people had written, and some of it seemed better than anything I could do. Instead of being inspired by the magazine work, I began to wonder whether I could really ever hope to be a writer at all. The little I managed to write seemed to fall into a crack—not quite poetry, not quite prose. I began to imagine myself, a failed writer, locked into a house with six kids—a fat housewife reading movie magazines and gobbling chocolate creams.

When I wasn't in class, doing homework or reading other people's writing, there always seemed to be a meeting, decisions to make, votes to take. What would we call the magazine? How many issues would we print? How much would we charge? What color paper? What kind of type? How many poems, how much prose? Marty and Mr. Justin chose to use linoleum block prints for the artwork, and Miss Hamilton started the art students working on designs. Marty would choose designs, coordinate them, and design the cover. We began to wonder how such a little magazine could be so much work.

For a week and a half after the picnic I was so involved with the magazine that there never seemed to be time for anything else. Even my sixteenth birthday came and went with scarcely a moment's notice. Mom was sick and couldn't come, so we decided to celebrate over Thanksgiving; Marty gave me a new, leather-bound journal; Chuck sent flowers.

Marty had taken her plans to the Penwomen meeting and then seemed to be as involved in the artwork as I was in the editorial choices. At least she was spending as much time in the studio as I was in meetings. We didn't talk much about what we were doing. I knew that once the magazine was ready for the printer, everything would ease up. Father Purdy had asked us to have it ready to sell at the Altar Guild's Christmas Bazaar, so we were working against an earlier deadline than we'd expected.

Then one evening during study hall, as I was checking my calendar to see how long I had to finish a paper for English, I saw that Halloween, with its costume party, was Saturday, only three days away. I hadn't even thought about a costume. Marty was stretched across her bed, reading her chemistry book.

"Halloween's Saturday," I said, thinking she had probably forgotten too.

"I know," she said, without looking up from her reading.

"You want to do a costume together? Maybe we can get Scovie to go with us and be a water molecule. You want to be oxygen or hydrogen?"

Marty looked up. "I can't. I'm working with Sylva."

"Sylva Hart?"

"Is there another?" She sat up. "She asked me if I'd help

her with her costume. And then she had an idea for both of us. We're going as Mary and Martha."

"Mary and Martha? You don't mean the Bible Mary and Martha?"

"Why not? We just did that section about them in religion class."

"Well, for one thing, what're you going to do for costumes? One wear makeup and the other not? How the heck can you go as Mary and Martha?"

The old gleam was in Marty's eyes. "That's the whole point. How do you take two sisters and show the difference? It has to be subtle—there would be the family resemblance but still that difference in their personalities. Mr. Justin gave me the idea. I'm doing papier-mâché masks. It's like sculpture, really. Did you know that masks are among the oldest art forms?"

"Yeah, way back to the first witch doctors."

"That's part of what makes it fun. To take masks, used in all sorts of primitive religions, and do Christian ones. Anyway, I decided the main difference between the two had to be color. So I'm using lots of grays and blues in Martha and lots of pink in Mary. Martha gets a gray robe—that's what Sylva's doing— and Mary gets red." She grinned. "I'll be Martha, of course. Come to the studio tomorrow and see the masks. They're almost done."

"But why Bible characters?"

"Sylva's going to join the Altar Guild this Sunday, and she thought since Halloween started out as a religious occasion, we could tie it all together. You know how Father Purdy is about the Altar Guild. I think she's trying to impress him. But it's been great fun doing the masks, so why not?"

Marty had always thought the Altar Guild was too pretentious, too obviously pious. Joining the Guild was one sure way of proving what a good Turnbull girl you were. This was the first time I'd ever heard her mention it without some sort of snide remark.

"It can't be easy to fit in when you come as a junior, you know. Sylva hasn't been accepted very well. Remember how Scovie reacted? Joining the Guild will give her a sort of ready-made group. Anyway, it can't hurt."

"I guess not." I couldn't get over the feeling that I'd been left out. "Why didn't you tell me about the masks before? How long have you been working on them?"

"I started sometime after the picnic—sure, it was after the picnic that she first asked if I'd help her make a costume. I didn't tell you about them because you've been so busy with the magazine. Anyway, you never asked me what I've been doing in the studio all this time, either—or come to see, for that matter."

"I guess I just thought you were working on the magazine too."

"Mike, you are positively obsessed. Like I was about the windows, remember?"

"I suppose so. But what'll I do for a costume?"

"Why not go as a poet? How about Sylvia Plath? You could carry a model oven."

"Marty, that's awful!"

"Sorry. Millay, then. You still like her, don't you? A Twenties costume wouldn't be too hard, and you can take her *Complete Works* in case nobody can figure out who you are."

And so I had a costume of sorts in time for the party. When Marty and Sylva won the award for most original costume, I tried to tell myself it didn't bother me. Still, after that the party wasn't much fun. And when I heard Father Purdy tell Stoney how refreshing it was to see a religious idea at a party full of witches and clowns, the bite of doughnut I'd just taken turned to sawdust in my mouth. I took Millay's poetry into a corner of the gym and read "Renascence" right through the apple bobbing.

Marty was supposed to go to the Penwomen meeting with me the next afternoon, but as I was gathering up my folder of magazine materials, she came into the room, still dressed for church, and handed me the sketches the art students had handed in. "Can you take these for me, Mike? I've promised Sylva I'd help her get ready for the Altar Guild's induction ceremony this evening. She's really nervous."

"But you're the art editor. Everybody's expecting a whole report."

"There's nothing special to tell them. Just show them these. The ones Justin and I want to use are marked with a checkmark on the front, and the poem or whatever each one is to be used with is on the back. If they want to make any changes, you can tell me what they are."

"What about the cover design? Have you got it finished?"

Marty shook her head. "I've been too busy with those masks."

I couldn't remember a time Marty had simply backed out on a commitment. "You've known about this meeting all week."

"Mike, it isn't that important! I'll do the cover this week!"

And she was gone, leaving me with my folder in one hand and the drawings in the other. She was right, I knew. It didn't matter who took the drawings over. So why was I furious?

When I got back from the meeting that day, Scovie was sitting on my bed, nibbling at her fingernails. I put away the magazine materials and smacked her hand. "I thought you'd quit biting your nails in the eighth grade!"

She looked surprised. "I didn't even know I was doing it."

"Well, what's up?"

"It's that damned roommate of mine."

"What's the matter now?"

"I *have* tried, Mike. I really have!"

"I believe you."

"But she's getting weirder by the hour."

I waited for her to go on. She was biting at her thumbnail again.

"You know she's joining the Altar Guild tonight."

"Sure." If there was one thing I knew about Sylva, it was that.

"And every single day this week she's gone to early Mass. Including Saturday!"

"What's the matter with that?"

"First of all, she sets her alarm to go off practically in the middle of the night, then she doesn't turn it off until it's almost run down. Then she goes stomping around the room, tripping over the end of my bed, getting dressed. By the time she leaves, I'm so wide awake it might as well be noon!"

"Can't you ask her to be quieter? Or to dress in the bath-room or something?"

"It isn't just that. I really mean it that the whole thing is weird, and joining the Altar Guild is about the weirdest thing of all. When she first got here, she bitched about even having to go to regular chapel and take religion classes. She refused to say the Creed or the Lord's Prayer or anything. She said she was an atheist and that Turnbull was violating her civil rights. It was a very big thing!"

"Did Father Purdy convert her or something?"

"If he did, it had to be a sudden miracle. One minute she

was an atheist, the next minute the room was full of prayer books and there were those elegantly lettered Bible quotations all over her bulletin board. I mean it, Mike, I've never seen anything like it. Next thing you know, she'll be wanting to put up a shrine in our room—*my* room!"

"Marty thinks she just wants to join the Guild so she'll have a group to belong to. We haven't made it exactly easy for her to be part of the class."

Scovie frowned. "It hasn't been any harder for her than for anybody else. Did Marty get her off on this kick?"

"No way. Marty hates the Altar Guild. And you've heard her on the subject of Father Purdy! Besides, I don't think she'd even talked to Sylva much until they did that Mary-Martha thing at Halloween. And that was Sylva's idea. I'd be willing to bet Marty doesn't know Sylva ever called herself an atheist."

Scovie glanced at her watch and jumped up. "I've got to get to the kitchen. I don't know what's with Sylva, Mike, but I don't like living with some kind of Jesus freak."

As Scovie left, she passed Marty in the hall without a word.

"What's the matter with Scovie?" Marty asked.

I was surprised to see Marty was still in her good clothes. "Nothing much," I said. "Sylva's religious kick is getting on her nerves."

Marty took a pair of jeans and a sweater out and began to change. "I'd hardly call it a 'kick.' Sylva's whole family is close to the church. Her uncle's a priest and she has a cousin who's a nun. When her parents split, she was sent here because of the church connection."

I was getting thoroughly tired of the whole subject. "Did you get her ready for the Guild ceremony?"

"She's going to be okay. I told her I'd come along to give her some moral support."

"What kind of moral support does she need to go up to the altar rail and get a Guild veil?"

"You know that speech they have to give about why the Altar Guild is important to them—that's what has her so nervous. She says she'll feel better if she knows I'm out there when she makes her speech." Marty pulled on her sweater and took a silver chain out from under the turtle neck. On the chain was a small crucifix, the figure of Christ in relief, done with what looked like droplets of pewter. "Sylva gave me this to thank me for making the masks." She arranged it against the front of her sweater. "What do you think?"

"I think it's a pretty classy thank-you for a papier-mâché mask!"

"That's what I told her. Ordinarily, I wouldn't wear a crucifix anyway. But this one reminds me a little of the St. Mark's windows. It's so abstract, it's more like a contemporary cross. Her cousin—the nun—gave it to her."

"And she gave it to you? I don't understand."

"Sylva's had a really hard time, Mike. Even before her parents got into that divorce mess, things were rough on her at home. She really didn't have anybody, except for one friend at school. And then she had to leave and come here where there was absolutely no one. Scovie hasn't helped much, you know. She just needs to feel she's got a friend here. How could I turn it down?"

How indeed. "A noble gesture!" I said.

But all during supper that night I could hardly keep my eyes off that crucifix.

After school a few days later, I was sitting in the room reading a letter from Chuck. The Hockey Dance was coming up again, and we were going together. I wouldn't have called his letter a love letter, but something was definitely changing between us. Over the summer he'd written about the things he was doing, griped about his job and his father. This letter was less about what was going on at Southport and more about how often he thought about me, how much he was looking forward to the dance. Could he come visit over Thanksgiving vacation; could he come up to Turnbull some Sunday afternoon and take me out for dinner? He didn't go so far as to protest his passion, but I thought it was about as close as Chuck could get to it. I was suddenly looking forward to the dance, too. As I was reading the letter for the third time, Marty and Sylva came in.

"I thought you had an editorial board meeting," Marty said.

"Not today. A whole day without a meeting!"

"Amazing." Marty sat down at her desk, and Sylva plunked herself in the middle of Marty's bed.

"Isn't there a class hockey practice?" I asked Sylva. She was playing left wing on the class team, the same position she'd had on varsity.

"I dropped out," she said. "It was taking too much time."

I wondered what it was taking time from, but I didn't say anything. No wonder Scovie had been in a foul mood all day. Dropping the team didn't seem to be a very good way of making friends in the class. "How's the magazine cover coming?"

Marty avoided my eyes. "I haven't really gotten going on it yet. I've been busy."

Busy? I couldn't imagine what she'd been busy at. Several times I'd checked at the studio to see if she might be there working on the cover, but she hadn't been there. "You working on another project?"

She glanced at Sylva, and I thought some kind of secret seemed to be passing between them in that look. "Paranoid," I thought. But I couldn't get it out of my mind.

"I guess you could say that." I waited for an explanation, but none came.

"I got another letter from Chuck." I felt as if I were talking to a stranger, having to work at conversation. "He wants to take me out for dinner some Sunday."

"Sounds like fun."

"You have a date for the Hockey Dance yet?" I asked her. Chuck had given me the names of a couple of cadets who were interested in art and I'd given them to Marty. We thought that might at least solve the usual blind date problems.

"I'm not going," she said.

"What?" I looked at her and she looked away. "Are you kidding?" I almost reminded her of last spring, but didn't. Maybe she didn't want Sylva to know about all that.

"Would I kid about a thing like that?"

"But I got you those names! Chuck says they're all okay guys!"

"I just don't want to go through all that first-date hassle again."

"What's the point, anyway?" Sylva asked. "What kind of guy goes to a military academy?"

I thought about Chuck and why he was at Southport. "What kind of girl goes to a boarding school?" If I'd expected some sort of reaction from Marty, some sign that I'd scored a point for our side, I didn't get it. She was suddenly very interested in the top of her desk. I turned to Sylva. "I suppose you aren't going either."

Sylva smiled. "No. There are better ways to spend an evening than listening to some adolescent boy trying to be impressive."

Marty stood up. "See you later, Mike. We're going to the

chapel for a while." Sylva got up and went past Marty into the hall. When she got to the door, Marty stopped and looked back at me. "I'm joining the Altar Guild," she said and went out, shutting the door as if she were putting up a barrier before I could respond.

I just sat there, staring at the closed door. What was happening?

At the next Penwomen meeting Miss Engles told me Marty had skipped her Saturday session with Mr. Justin and asked if I knew why. "She didn't even call to explain," she said.

☙ S I X T E E N ☙

"I forgot," Marty said when I asked her why she had skipped her art lesson.

She was sitting on her bed, already in her pajamas, though it was still an hour till lights out, running a brush through her hair. She didn't look at me when she said it. In fact, I realized, she hadn't looked at me directly all evening. It was almost as if she weren't really in the room with me at all. I knew how impossible it would have been for the Marty I knew to forget an art lesson. Where had she been? What had she been doing? How could she sit there so calmly, telling me what I knew couldn't be true?

"She doesn't care whether I believe her or not," I thought. I was reminded of the Princess those first weeks at Turnbull. She was all icy elegance, all poise and reserve. I felt as if I had to make some kind of connection, get her to look at me, at least. A small, black leather book lay next to her on the bed. "A new prayer book?" I asked.

She looked at it, her eyes taking a moment to register, then she smiled. "St. Augustine's Prayer Book."

"New?"

"It's Sylva's," she said, and her smile got brighter. "You

should read the devotions on the Stations of the Cross! There's so much feeling in them."

"Like your windows," I said, hoping that I could get her off religion and onto art.

"Better," she said. "My windows were—well, not as concerned with God as with art. I was so busy trying to work out the technique that I missed the spiritual quality, I'm afraid."

"The St. Mark's board didn't think so."

"They were doing the same thing—thinking about the decoration of their church, that's all." She dismissed the biggest achievement of her life and picked up the prayer book, opening it to a page near the front. "Listen to this. It's the beginning of St. Augustine's Collect. 'They that be wise shall shine as the brightness of the firmament; and they that turn many to righteousness as the stars for ever and ever.'"

"What does that mean?"

She smiled again, a smile that didn't seem to go past her mouth. "It means that anyone who can lead people to God, anyone who can turn them on to the Truth, will shine like a star. Like St. Augustine, for instance. Or Father Purdy."

That was too much. "Marty! You said Father Purdy knew more about wine than about people. What's starlike about him? You said his religion classes were likely to turn people *away* from God."

"I could never see past the person, Mike. I was so busy disliking the *man* that I didn't see beyond him to God. No matter how weak a person is, no matter how bad, God can work through him. Anybody can witness for the truth. Anybody can be a shining star. You just have to sacrifice whatever makes you separate. You have to give up whatever gets between you and God, then God can work with you and through you."

Scovie was right. Whatever was going on was weird. I could hardly believe this was Marty. Sylva had been working on her, and suddenly everything I'd known about her seemed to have disappeared. I couldn't avoid any longer what I'd been wanting to tell her.

"Marty, Sylva was an atheist when she came here. An atheist! This religion thing isn't real with her!"

Marty looked at me then, her eyes cold and hard and unrecognizable. "You've been listening to Scovie, haven't you? Scovie would say anything to hurt Sylva. She did that to you last year; I should think you'd have learned." She paused, and I could hear my heart beating in my ears. "You can tell her it won't work, Mike. God knows the truth."

"At least somebody does," I thought. But I said nothing. There was nothing to say.

Marty covered a yawn with one hand. "I've got to get to sleep," she said. "Six o'clock comes early."

I nodded. Six o'clock was an hour earlier than anyone except a fanatic had to get up, but she'd been cleared of that charge once. She knelt beside her bed to say her prayers, something she'd been doing only since she'd joined the Altar Guild. Then she turned out her light, pulled up her blankets, and turned away. I sat at my desk, wishing I could talk to Miss Engles. I'd tried once before, but she'd been busy, and then I'd decided it was just as well. What could I say? That Sylva was making Marty more religious? It hardly seemed a reason to condemn a person. Anyway, I had a pretty good idea of what Miss Engles would say. She'd remind me of Sylva's sad story and point out that I was acting like a jealous roommate. "No relationship is easy or safe or certain," she'd said. It hadn't seemed to apply to friends.

I'd gotten used to Marty's alarm going off at six and scarcely noticed it anymore. But the next morning, while it was still dark in the room, I found myself suddenly awake. I tried to think what had wakened me, but I couldn't. The luminous dial on my clock said five thirty, so I knew it couldn't have been Marty's alarm. Then I saw that there was someone in the room, standing next to Marty's bed. It was Sylva.

"Marty!" she whispered, shaking Marty's shoulder. "Wake up. It's me."

Marty turned over, grumbling, until she saw who it was. "Sylva! Did I forget to set my clock?"

"No. I'm early. I couldn't sleep, so I finally got dressed instead of waiting for the alarm to ring."

Marty sat up and rubbed her eyes. "I'll get up too. We can go to chapel early and meditate."

"No, it's too cold! They don't start the heat until six or so. There are practically icicles growing in the hall. I'm frozen!" She sat on the bed, rubbing her arms and shivering.

"You want a sweater?" Marty asked, and started to get up to get her one.

"No, you stay warm. The heat'll come on soon." She shivered some more. "Maybe I could just crawl under the blanket till it's time to get up. I can't imagine why I couldn't sleep."

Marty flung her covers back, and Sylva crawled into bed beside her. "Ah, that's better. Thanks. I thought I'd never be warm again."

I lay there listening, but they were whispering so quietly now that I couldn't hear what they were saying. And after a while I went to sleep in spite of myself. Marty's alarm didn't go off, and when I woke with the rising bell, they were gone. I didn't know what to think. It could have been perfectly true.

Sylva could have had trouble sleeping. It *was* cold in the dorm before the heat came on. It was perfectly reasonable to want to stay warm until time for chapel. But there was another whole set of possibilities that I didn't even want to think about. So I didn't. I got up and dressed and went to breakfast and did my best not to think at all.

Over the next few days Marty began going to bed earlier and earlier. I knew she couldn't be finishing her homework, let alone doing any artwork. She seemed to move from chapel to classes and back to chapel again, with no interest in anything else. Her eyes became almost opaque, her face a kind of zombie mask. There wasn't anything I could say or do. She was barely speaking to me.

Marty quit using her alarm, so I no longer knew when she was getting up. By the time the rising bell rang, she would be gone. Then one morning I woke up before the rising bell. The room was dark, but not so dark that I couldn't see that there were two people in Marty's bed. And then I heard their voices, barely whispering. I knew it was what I hadn't even been able to admit to myself I might find. But listening to them whispering, occasionally giggling, I was sure I'd known all along. It explained why Marty had stopped using her alarm. I wondered how long Sylva had been there.

Then I realized what had awakened me. I had to go to the bathroom. If I got up, they'd know I knew Sylva was there. I didn't want that. It was as if by not admitting I'd seen them I could make it less real. So I curled up in a tight little ball and lay very still, trying to will away the need to go. It wouldn't go away. Finally, as quietly as I could, I got out of bed and tiptoed to the door. I hoped if I could make it look as if I weren't quite awake they'd think I hadn't seen them. When I got back to the room, Sylva was sitting on Marty's bed, dressed in her class uniform. I paid no attention to them, just crawled back into bed and pulled up the covers as if I were still half asleep.

While Marty dressed and got her prayer books, I pretended to be asleep. But I could no more have gone back to sleep than I could have walked on water. Every muscle in my body felt as if it had been stretched on a rack. When they left, I lay there till the rising bell, my mind whirling. What could I say? Who could I talk to? I had to have help from somewhere.

But then I remembered last spring and knew I couldn't tell anyone. How could I let it start all over again? This time I wouldn't have the comfort of knowing it wasn't true. I didn't know what *was* true. I didn't want to know. I was just plain scared.

That evening Marty studied in the library instead of in our room. When she got back, she put on her pajamas, brushed her hair, said her prayers, and got into bed, never so much as looking in my direction. I didn't exist. I set my mental alarm to wake me early, but it never had a chance. At five o'clock I felt a tap on my shoulder and found Scovie standing next to my bed in her robe and slippers, shivering.

"Where are they?" she asked.

It was as if an enormous weight had been taken off my shoulders. Somebody else knew. There was finally somebody I could talk to. I sat up in bed and turned on my reading light. "I don't know. I'd have thought they'd be in your room."

Scovie shook her head. "Sylva hasn't been in her own bed after midnight or so for three nights at least."

"She's been here."

Scovie sat on my bed, then, heavily—as if her legs had given out on her. "You mean they've, they've . . ."

I nodded. Scovie's face was set like a mask. "I knew from the minute Sylva arrived she was trouble. But I never thought it would be this."

I tried to think of all those justifications—Sylva's hard time at home, her loneliness, her insecurities. It wasn't enough.

"Shouldn't we tell somebody?" Scovie asked.

"Tell them what? What do we *know?*"

"But if they've been sleeping together . . ."

"What do we *know?*"

Scovie chewed at her thumbnail for a moment. "It would be like last year, you mean?" I didn't bother answering and after a moment she nodded. "I guess you're right. What good would it do, anyway?"

I wished I could think of some other way. More than anything I wanted—needed—to talk to somebody. We padded around the cold halls then, looking for them, but we couldn't find them anywhere. When they appeared at breakfast, Scovie just shook her head at me and shrugged.

✺ ✺

At the Penwomen meeting Sunday I sat through all the usual enthusiasms about the magazine. It didn't seem to matter much anymore. Miss Hamilton had told Miss Engles that most of the linoleum blocks were finished or nearly finished. The dummy was coming along so well I could report that we would beat the printer's deadline.

Then someone asked about the cover. I just sat there.

"I said, what about the cover? We haven't even seen a sketch yet."

I opened my mouth to say something and stopped. What could I tell them? That the art editor, my own roommate, hadn't even shown *me* a sketch? That she hadn't spoken to me for days? I just sat with my mouth open and my hands clasped on my folder.

Miss Engles rescued me, saying that the cover was the last thing we needed and that we could be sure it would be worth waiting for. Then someone was reading a new poem, and the subject of the magazine was closed. It was as if everyone in the room had simply vanished, leaving me alone in the red chair with a vision of Marty's empty bed. Scovie and I hadn't been able to find out where they'd been, but neither Marty nor Sylva had spent a whole night in their own beds since Thursday.

When the meeting was over, I didn't move from the chair while everyone else gathered up coats. Miss Engles stood at the door, saying good-bye to each girl, until they had all gone. Then she closed the door and turned back to me.

"Are you ready to tell me about it?" she asked.

I shook my head, wanting more than anything in the world to tell her and knowing I couldn't. It was as if suddenly I didn't know how I felt about anything, even how I felt about her.

"I'm sorry I couldn't see you the other day."

"That's all right. It wasn't—I'm not writing anymore anyway." I stood up then, and my folder fell to the floor.

As I knelt to gather up the papers, Miss Engles spoke. "Marty didn't go for her art lesson again yesterday. John told me last night. He's very worried. He hasn't heard from her in two weeks."

I kept trying to gather up my papers, and they kept slipping away from me.

"He thought he'd speak to Miss Stonehill about her."

"No!" I almost shouted. "Tell him not to talk to Stoney yet. Please!"

I managed to get everything into my arms, grabbed my jacket, and ran out of the apartment and down the stairs, the world blurring around me as I ran. I was aware of Miss Engles calling my name, but I didn't turn around. I never even stopped to put on my jacket. When I got to the dorm, I couldn't go in. I set my folder by the door, shoved my arms into my jacket sleeves, and went back out through the growing dusk toward the breakwater.

There was a brisk, cold wind off the lake, churning the gray water into white caps, the waves sending spray up and over the rocks so that I had to sit far back. I hadn't worn a hat, and my ears began to ache with the cold, but still I sat there, my head on my knees, trying to sort things out.

Apparently, Miss Engles had been seeing Mr. Justin. What Marty had predicted at the picnic seemed to be happening. The picnic. What had happened that day?

And where did it all leave me? I had Chuck, of course. The dance was less than a week away. But what did I really have with him? I'd been in a girls' school since I was thirteen, and Chuck was the only boy I'd ever dated. I was sixteen years old! By this time Bits had had who knows how many relationships with boys. It was practically all she thought about. Was something the matter with me? With the rest of us? Willie and Scovie were jocks. I knew all the jokes about lady jocks. I thought about Tag and her science fiction. She'd understood about Bits and Donald Kincaid, but when had I ever heard her talk about guys herself? What kind of a person was a Turnbull girl anyway? Was Bits the only one of us who was normal?

And Marty. My best friend. I thought about the letters all summer, the afternoons at the beach, the sharing of whatever it was that made her draw and me write. What had happened to all that? She'd always been able to make it alone, I'd always known that. But I'd thought she needed me, too, at least a little.

What had she seen in Sylva? And what was happening between them now? Was Sylva gay? Was Marty? I thought about friendship, about loyalty. Maybe I was letting *her* down. I'd never been able to share her feeling about religion. Maybe she needed someone to understand that part of her too. Maybe I could do something even now. If I could just talk to her, get her to listen long enough. . . .

Suddenly, a wave, larger than the ones before it, hit the base of the rocks with a crash that sent a wall of icy water over me. The cold was so unexpected, so intense, it took my breath away and left me shaking. I pulled my sodden jacket around me and started back to the dorm, tripping and stumbling as I went. The shock of the water must have stopped my mind as suddenly as it had stopped my breath. I was back in my room putting on dry clothes before I knew it. Marty wasn't there.

As I was pulling on my moccasins, having set my shoes on the radiator to dry out, Mrs. Martin, our dorm mother, knocked politely on the door and stuck her head around it.

"Michelle," she began, then stepped inside. "I've been trying to find you for some time. Your roommate and Sylva Hart have made an unusual request. I've already spoken to Barbara about it, but I need your reaction as well."

It took me a moment to realize that she meant Scovie; Mrs. Martin doesn't believe in nicknames. But then I knew what she was going to say.

"They've asked permission to change roommates. They both go to early Mass, and have been most unhappy at disturbing you each morning with their early alarm bells."

I didn't want to hear any more, but I nodded. I might as well know what she was going to say.

"And we all know how miserable Barbara's been, having to share such a small room. They've graciously suggested that they take the small room and let you and Barbara have this one. They pointed out that you roomed together your first two years here, so it wouldn't be like breaking in a new room-mate."

I nodded again.

"It seems to be a perfectly reasonable idea, and one they presented with such unselfish reasons, I could hardly turn them down if you and Barbara agree. As I say, I've already spoken to her, and she's given her approval."

I started to say something, but nothing came out. I cleared my throat and managed to get out a sound that could be inter-preted as affirmative. Mrs. Martin smiled her polite, birdlike little smile and went out. I wondered what she would say if she knew what really lay behind that "unselfish" request.

For a moment I considered going back to Miss Engles' apart-ment and telling her everything. But what I really wanted was to have her hold on to me and let me cry. I couldn't go to her of all people. So I sat on my bed, staring past my reflection into the darkness outside the window until the supper bell rang.

Marty and Sylva skipped supper. When I came back to the room afterward, Marty's things were already gone.

❧ SEVENTEEN ❧

Scovie moved in that night. When she'd put everything away, we sat on the beds, not talking, not quite looking at each other. Finally, Scovie started working on some homework, but I couldn't seem to concentrate on anything. We won't talk about it, I realized. We know and we don't know. And anyway, it's too close. Too frightening. So she worked while I sat, my journal open in front of me, and stared at the door of the room.

The next morning when I got up there was a note on my desk, from Marty. I opened it, my hands trembling at the sight of my name in that familiar handwriting.

"Dear Michelle," it began. I skipped down to the end and saw that she'd signed it *Martha*, not *The Masked Gladiator* as she'd always signed her letters. "I don't write this to hurt you, believe me. There's too much pain between people in this world as it is. I thought I knew all about God, all about what He wanted of me. Sylva has shown me how wrong I was. She's shown me how important it is to keep God first in my life. I've always thought of my art as a gift from God, but even that gift has gotten in the way, because I let it become more important to me than God Himself. Until I can find a way to keep Him first, I have to give up whatever interferes. That means my art, of course, and you too. Please don't try to communicate with me about this. There's nothing to say.

"I haven't always been truthful with you—or even with myself. I know now that my feelings for Priscilla were just what everyone said they were. But I know myself now, and I know that if I'm to save what little good there is, I have to keep God first."

I read it again, feeling so dizzy I had to hold on to the edge of my desk. Then I took it into the bathroom, tore it into tiny pieces, and flushed it away. Another wave of dizziness swept over me and I vomited, flushed again, and vomited again, until there was nothing left, and I was just holding myself over the bowl while my stomach heaved as if it would tear me apart.

Someone must have heard me because there were people around me then, and I was being helped down the hall toward the room, Mrs. Martin twittering about getting me to the infirmary. The next thing I knew I was being tucked into a white iron bed by the school nurse and a thermometer was being pushed into my mouth. It didn't seem worth it to argue. I could hardly tell them it was a note that had made me sick, a note I'd flushed away along with everything that came afterward. I lay in bed all morning, as disconnected as if I'd been drugged.

Scovie came in to see me sometime, probably lunch hour, and then just stood there, not saying anything. I shook my head at her and turned toward the wall. She must have left; I must have slept, because the next thing I remember is the nurse bringing me a supper tray of soup and crackers that looked about as appetizing as what I'd flushed down the toilet. She asked me some questions which I would have answered except that my voice wasn't working again. Then she tried to get me to eat the soup, but I just turned my head away.

"This will pass," I thought to myself. "I'll be okay in the morning. There's nothing the matter with me at all, so it has to go away. I just lost a friend, is all. It isn't the end of the world." All I wanted to do was sleep.

But all night my sleep was torn by nightmares. Miss Engles and Marty seemed to be floating round and round the bed. Then Chuck would be there, shaking his head. Then Sylva. "I did it!" she would say. "Less than a month! Less than a month!" It wasn't quite like a dream, though, because I didn't seem to be asleep, and even my nightmares usually have some sort of story to them. This was just a series of images, over and over. By morning, I was more tired than when I'd gone to sleep. They brought in the school's consulting doctor, who took my temperature and my blood pressure and looked in my throat and ears and went out with the nurse, shaking his head.

Later, Father Purdy came in. I remember thinking how right Marty had been about him. This was not a person who could help. He sat on the metal folding chair by the bed, puffing on his pipe and looking uncomfortable. I wanted to tell him it was all right, and then I thought how silly it was for me to think of comforting him. What was he there for, anyway? Finally he cleared his throat and asked if anything was bothering me. I'd have laughed if I'd had the energy, but I just shook my head. He looked relieved. After a quick prayer of some kind—I wasn't in the mood to listen to anything that had to do with God—he went away.

There was lunch sometime, but I didn't eat that either. The nurse kept coming in to look at me, her face getting more serious every time. But I couldn't bring myself to care. I just kept slipping off to sleep again, just a peaceful darkness now. I felt as if I'd never wake up.

Eventually, I opened my eyes and saw that the room was dark. It must be supper time, I knew. My stomach felt hollow and empty, but I couldn't put that together with hunger, somehow. Suddenly, the light went on over my head, and I blinked in the brightness. There was a person standing by the door, a tray in her hands. After another blink or two I saw it wasn't the nurse; it was Miss Engles. She brought the tray over, set it on the table next to the bed, and sat down in the chair Father Purdy had sat in. She didn't say a word, just reached out and took my hand. I wanted to jerk it back, but hers was so warm, the only thing I had been sure was real in so long, I didn't move.

"Is it possible to hurt to death?" I asked, surprised to find my voice working again. It sounded like an incredibly stupid question, once it was out in the air like that.

Miss Engles didn't laugh. "I thought so once. There may even be times when you wish it were. But pain goes away if you give it time. It leaves scars, but it does go."

"Do you know what I'm talking about?"

"Yes. Marty sent John a note."

I tried to sit up, then sank back onto the pillow. "Did she tell him she was sacrificing her art to God?"

"Something like that. Her reasoning wasn't very clear."

"There isn't any reasoning. Those are all Sylva's words."

"She's hiding behind them right now. She has to have something."

"It isn't God."

Miss Engles shook her head slowly. "No. And I don't think even Marty really thinks it is."

"What are you going to do?"

She helped me sit up, fluffed my pillow, and put my supper tray in front of me. "If you mean about Marty and Sylva, nothing for the moment. John called Priscilla this afternoon, and she's coming here as soon as she can get away."

I sat up straighter, spilling some of the soup on my tray. "She can't. She'd only make it worse. Marty said in her note— she said—" And again I couldn't say the words out loud.

"That what people said about them last year was true?"

I nodded, put a napkin on the spilled soup, and watched the reddish broth soak into the cloth.

"Priscilla told John she might say that. Nothing happened between them, Mike. But Marty's listening to Sylva. When she remembers how she felt about Priscilla, she's remembering from a new point of view."

I thought about sitting on the breakwater that night, however long ago it had been, and the questions I'd been asking myself about my own feelings, for Marty, for Miss Engles. I thought I could understand.

"You've always been jealous of Marty," Miss Engles said. Before I had a chance to protest, she went on. "You've always admired her control, her ability to ignore what people thought, or said, about her."

I nodded.

"But in some ways, Marty's more vulnerable than you. She's been so busy keeping herself safe from any damage from the outside, that when she began to distrust herself she was as cut off from help as she'd ever been from being hurt."

I took a sip of soup. It was vegetable soup, hot and comforting. The hollow feeling in my stomach became hunger, and I took another sip.

"Good," Miss Engles said. "Right now I want you to get yourself out of here. You won't do anyone any good in here."

"I don't think it's as easy as that," I said, and the feeling of separation began coming back, seeming to pull her, the room, even the supper tray, away on to another plane.

Her voice sounded as if it had to come a long way. "I didn't say it was easy. But you have to begin somewhere. Begin with your soup."

I wanted to explain how I felt, but I didn't know how. It was as if I'd looked down at what I thought was solid ground I was standing on and found nothing but air. Like a cartoon character, all I could do when I noticed it was fall. I'd built everything on what I'd thought was real, friendship, loyalty, art. Now they sounded naive and stupid. And if I didn't know anything about Marty, what did I know about me?

"Marty was my friend," I said.

"Yes. But she's a separate person. When it comes down to it, she can't choose her way according to how it will affect you. Her choices have to grow out of who she is. Don't ask more of friendship than it can give."

A question seemed to come out of nowhere, and before I could even think, I asked it. "Do you love John Justin?"

She didn't even blink. "I'm not sure, Mike. I may."

I don't know what my face must have told her, but I know how I felt. As if the bottom of something had dropped out.

"I'm sorry if it seems that everyone's deserting you. But don't start worrying about whether you're feeling jealous. People can be jealous for a lot of reasons. Perhaps if I hadn't been so involved with John in the last few weeks, I'd have noticed what was happening. But I, too, am a person." She sighed. "Don't put labels on anything quite yet, Mike."

I ate some of my soup then, and she took away the tray, tucked me in, turned out the light, and left. I lay there in the dark for a long time, thinking about what she'd said, wondering how Priscilla Kincaid could reach the Marty who had written that note. I knew I'd probably get up in the morning and get dressed and go to classes. But I still felt as if I were standing on air where there used to be rock.

❊ EIGHTEEN ❊

The rest of the week I managed to go to classes, make a half-hearted attempt at doing my homework, and get the magazine ready for the printer. Miss Hamilton, of all people, had designed a cover when she learned that Marty would not. That seemed ironic, but not quite ironic enough to be funny. I was so used to thinking Miss Hamilton's work wasn't any good that I was surprised to discover I liked her design. Maybe I'd been looking through Marty's eyes for too long. Or maybe, as Miss Engles suggested, Miss Hamilton had grown too. Nothing seemed to be the way I'd always thought things were. No one could be relied on anymore to be what I'd expected.

Marty and Sylva kept to themselves. I saw them in class, but partly I avoided noticing them and partly they avoided me. By the time I'd gotten out of the infirmary, they'd stopped going to chapel all the time. I didn't know if Marty had ever believed all that religious smokescreen or not, but now they didn't seem to need it anymore. I waited for people to notice, to start all the old talk again, but nothing happened. If anyone did see, did suspect the truth, no one was saying it out loud. Turnbull had suddenly become a very liberal place.

Saturday morning, the day of the tournament and the Hockey Dance, I skipped the games on the pretense of having a meeting with the printer and went downtown, just to get off campus. I spent an hour in a corner booth of a greasy spoon, nursing a cup of cocoa and a sweet roll I didn't want, watching people go in and out, half listening to the conversations at the tables around me. Then I walked back along Prospect Avenue as slowly as I dared, staring at the iron gray November lake. In a few hours Chuck would be there, and I didn't know how I felt about that. I wanted to see him, but not sitting and watching a hockey game. And not in a dining room full of people. I wasn't sure how I was going to greet him when he got off the bus because I had the feeling that the person he'd see wasn't the person he was expecting.

When he did arrive, he didn't seem to notice. The weather wasn't bad, just a little blustery, so we sat close together, holding hands, as we watched the juniors win the tournament easily. I hoped he would think my lack of enthusiasm had to do with the lopsided score. But he didn't seem to notice that, either. He talked and joked and got me talking, even laughing for the first time all week.

Several times during dinner he touched my hand as we talked, and I was aware of my skin, of his, as if there were an electric current moving between us. Then I wanted to get away from him, to hide in my room all evening. But I wanted to stay with him, too, to keep up that contact, keep him with me.

When the dance was nearly over, he pulled me into a corner of the gym and held me by both shoulders, facing him. His glasses reflected the tiny lights among the decorations overhead. "I don't know what it is, Mike. But something is different tonight." So he hadn't missed it after all. "Do you want me to come to Waterford over Thanksgiving?"

"Yes." Did I?

"Good. Because we both have to get away. I know I joke a

lot about Southport, but this stretch from September till Thanksgiving really is too long. I think we're both stir crazy."

"Is that what it is?"

"I don't know. What does a poor dumb cadet know about anything? I just want some time with you away from here and away from Southport, where we can just be together for a while, like last summer."

"I don't think we can go back to last summer."

He grinned. "That isn't *exactly* what I meant."

When it was time for the buses to leave, we were among the couples who managed to find a shadowy corner for a few minutes. And when I finally let go of his hand as he stepped up onto the bus, it was like pulling away from a bit of myself.

"Next week!" he said, and blew me a kiss. A moment later, he'd found a window and was waving. "Next week," he said so I could lip read. As the bus pulled away, he was making crazy faces and I was laughing, unaware of the cold as the wind swept across the parking lot.

"Michelle Caine, you're just out of the infirmary. You'll catch your death!" And then I did notice the wind as Mrs. Martin guided me firmly back to the dorm. By the time I'd reached the room, I realized I hadn't thought about Marty since the buses arrived.

As I was getting ready for bed, Scovie came in. "The fight is on!" she said.

"What fight?"

"Priscilla Kincaid and Sylva Hart!"

"Priscilla's here?"

Scovie grinned. "She arrived during the dance. The word is when Mrs. Kincaid came in to find Marty, Sylva stormed out of the dorm and hasn't been seen since. And to think my mother believes the real world never touches Turnbull Hall."

I wanted to make sure Scovie understood about Marty and Priscilla Kincaid. But then I knew I was thinking in the old ways, defending the Princess against other people's opinions. What was the point? And who was I to defend her, anyway?

That night I didn't sleep much. I finally got up, thinking I might be able to write in my journal, but just sat with my pen in my hand until I had to give up. I picked up a volume of Sylvia Plath's poetry, but put it down halfway through the first poem. I kept wondering if Priscilla had reached Marty, and if she had, how we'd face each other and survive the rest of the year. Finally, I lost myself in Millay's *Collected Poems*. At least her pain was cushioned in the rhymes and easy rhythms.

Sylva and Marty weren't at breakfast, nor could I see any sign of Mrs. Kincaid. They weren't in chapel either, though I couldn't remember Marty's ever having missed choral Mass before. Scovie caught my eye once during the service; I shrugged and wondered again what was going on.

As we came out of chapel, down the long corridor that led to the main building, I saw Miss Engles, in jeans and boots, waiting at the entrance to the dining room. For a moment, I was surprised. She wasn't usually in the building on Sunday. But as I got closer, I could see that her face was strained and very pale.

She took me by the arm and guided me into the little guest dining room off the main dining hall, closed the windowed door, and leaned on it. "Sit down, Mike."

I sat on one of the antique mahogany and silk chairs, scarcely daring to breathe. Whatever it was, I didn't think I wanted to hear it.

"Sylva's been taken to the hospital," she said, "A drug overdose."

The room seemed to spin once and right itself. Sylva, she'd

said. Not Marty. "Did she do it on purpose?" I asked. Surely Marty and Sylva hadn't been doing drugs.

"If you mean was the overdose an accident, no. She left a note for Marty. But if you mean did she really want to die, no one can answer that. Probably not even Sylva."

"She made sure she'd be found in time, I'll bet."

"That doesn't necessarily mean anything."

"Where's Marty?"

"She and Priscilla are with Miss Stonehill."

"Did Sylva do it because Priscilla came back?"

Miss Engles sighed. "Apparently. None of us understood just how unhappy Sylva was, how desperately she needed to establish a relationship."

"You mean how badly she needed to prove her power."

"Sometimes it's the same thing." She came and sat on the edge of the table next to me. "Priscilla took Marty to the art studio last night. No matter how Marty thinks she felt about Priscilla, it was the painting they shared. Priscilla thought if she could talk to Marty where they had worked together so often, she could help her get in touch with herself again."

"Did it work?"

"She thinks so. Marty finished her design for the magazine cover, anyway. They worked almost all night."

"And Sylva jumped to the wrong conclusions."

"Sylva knew no more about Priscilla or about art than Marty had told her. She figured she couldn't compete with that combination. She must have thought she'd lost everything."

"Is she going to be all right?" Did I really care?

"Yes. At least she isn't going to die."

"And Marty's cover will be on the magazine?" Could it be that somehow we could wipe it all away and be back where we'd been before?

"No." Miss Engles put a hand on my shoulder, and I just managed not to shrug it off. "Marty's leaving Turnbull. That's what she and Priscilla are talking to Miss Stonehill about now. They called Marty's father this morning, and he's given his permission for Marty to transfer to the Wellington Academy. Priscilla is making arrangements for her to start after Thanksgiving. They agree with Priscilla that Marty is special."

"Don't we all!" I wondered why, as much as my eyes burned, I wasn't crying. "Do they know the rest?"

"About Marty and Sylva? Why should they?"

"Would they want her at their school if they knew?"

"They want her at Wellington because she has exceptional talent. She's sixteen. What else can anyone say? We don't know what her future will be—or Sylva's either, for that matter. I warned you once about labels, remember?"

There was that sensation of things pulling away again. "Then I don't understand anything. If that isn't what the label means, what is?"

Miss Engles rubbed the back of her neck. For a moment, I thought she wasn't going to answer at all, but then she looked at me and those gray eyes seemed to go right through me again. "The trouble is, homosexuality is one area no one can be quite sure about. There are still more questions than there are answers. Some lesbians say they've known about themselves since they were children, that once you're gay you just *are*, and the only question then is whether you accept it or not. But others say you can be one thing with one person and another with someone else—or at some other time in your life. A label is just too simple.

"And if labels aren't a good idea in general, they're particularly bad at your age. The one thing we know for certain is that some kind of homosexual experience, sometimes it's physical, sometimes psychological, is natural—'normal,' Mike—during adolescence. It's part of figuring out who you are, a first step, with someone like yourself, before you take the chance of reaching out to the other sex."

I almost laughed. "Nobody told Bits that."

"Maybe she found out all by herself, long before Donald Kincaid."

"But what if this isn't just a 'normal' thing? What if Marty . . ." Why did I have such trouble with the words?

"All right. What if? If she'd had such a relationship with a boy, would you feel this way?"

"But she didn't! And I'm—at least I *was* her best friend!"

"And that's where the pain is coming from, Mike. I know this has made you question who you are, but what hurts much more is that your best friend betrayed you. I don't have any words to help you come to terms with that."

I remembered the way the year had begun, that perfect picnic, riding through the dusk eating apples. I remembered what Marty had said about October, about the loss of Eden being both an ending and a beginning. It *would* be a beginning for her, in the school she'd always wanted more than Turnbull. For me, it was just an ending. The end of part of me. Eden was over, and it hadn't lasted half long enough.

❦ EPILOGUE ❦

I saw Marty before she left. We stood in the hall, Marty holding her portfolio, just looking at each other. There was so much to say, and there was nothing. When the chauffeur came out of the room behind her with her suitcases, I said something like "Be seeing you," and she said something like "Sure," and I was standing in an empty hallway with footsteps echoing behind me.

When Sylva was ready to leave the hospital, her mother came and took her things away. I don't know where she went, if they sent her to another school somewhere. I don't want to know, any more than I want to try to understand her. It's just safer, for now, to hate her. Whatever that says about me, I do.

So now that small room is empty, and the door stays shut. Scovie could have moved back in, but she didn't. We're just here, Scovie and I. Not like we were before Marty came, not like the days of the D.E.T.s, but it's better than being alone.

The magazine is finished. When it went to the printer, I asked the editorial board if they wanted to take Marty's name off as art editor, since she ended up having almost nothing to do with it, but they let it stay. It has two poems of mine in it, so I could hardly refuse to keep a copy for myself, but I don't look at it much.

Chuck came to Waterford over Thanksgiving, and we'll be going to the Christmas Ball together at Southport. There's something good between us, all right, but I'm not sure how much I trust it. I admit it's a great comfort that he's male.

Miss Engles and Mr. Justin are going to be married this summer. She says I'll be as welcome in their home as I've always been in her apartment. I'm not afraid of how I feel about her anymore. Like art with Marty and Priscilla, I guess what there is between us is mostly poetry. Or maybe, as she says, there are more ways to love than there are labels.

Marty's at Wellington. She wrote once, to tell me how exciting it is to be in a place where art is allowed to be the center of everything instead of an extra. She didn't mention the boys there. At the end of the letter she put in a kind of apology. I read the letter and put it away. Maybe later I'll answer it, but not now.

For a while I read one of Millay's poems over and over:

> *Now goes under, and I watch it go under, the sun*
> *That will not rise again.*
> *Today has seen the setting, in your eyes*
> *cold and senseless as the sea,*
> *Of friendship better than bread . . .*

I thought that was true; it was how I felt. But I'm beginning to see that sometimes Millay was more poetic than honest, too. The sun does rise again.

I wasn't ready to lose that friendship, even if Marty was. But what's done is done, and the sun goes right on. I've started to write again, and Miss Engles says that's like eating the soup. A good first step.